Elliot Stone
and the Mystery of the Summer Vacation Sea Monster

by LP Chase
Illustrations by Carl DiRocco

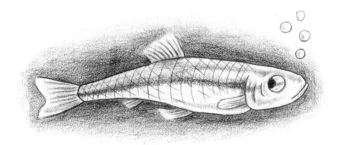

Blue Marlin Publications

D1377728

Blue Marlin Publications
823 Aberdeen Road
West Bay Shore, NY 11706

Text Copyright 2011 by LP Chase
Illustrations Copyright 2011 by Carl DiRocco
Cover Design by Carl DiRocco
Book Design & Layout by Jude Rich

First Edition: November 2011

ISBN13: 978-0-9792918-7-6

Library of Congress Cataloging-in-Publication Data

Chase, L. P., 1964-
  Elliot Stone and the mystery of the summer vacation sea monster /
L.P. Chase ; Illustrations by Carl DiRocco. -- 1st ed.
      p. cm.
  Summary: Having to leave his friends and miss a popular fourth-
grade graduation party, Elliot is not looking forward to spending
the summer in Vermont until he spots an unusual animal in Lake
Bomoseen.
  ISBN 978-0-9792918-7-6 (pbk. : alk. paper)
  1. Bomoseen, Lake (Vt.)--Juvenile fiction. [1. Bomoseen, Lake
(Vt.)--Fiction. 2. Sea monsters--Fiction. 3. Friendship--Fiction. 4.
Vacations--Fiction. 5. Mystery and detective stories.] I. DiRocco,
Carl, 1963- ill. II. Title.
  PZ7.C38734El 2011
  [Fic]--dc23
                    2011027616

Printed and bound in China by Regent Publishing Services, Ltd.
November 2011
Job # 111550

Acknowledgements

There are a few people to whom I owe a great deal of thanks. First and foremost, I'd like to thank my husband, Steve, for his unending reserve of off-the-cuff ideas that spontaneously grow into full-blown, amazing plots – every single time. I hope your idea pool never dries up. I could use a few more.

I'd also like to thank some of my critique group friends: Lisa Reiss, Karen Cleveland, and Linda Lodding, who have spent tireless days helping me perfect my work, and who've made me laugh during those stressful days of writer's block when I was sure my writing career was over. My craft wouldn't be where it is today without the motivation of these creative, talented writers.

A manuscript isn't complete without a set of hawk eyes checking it over for minute mistakes, which is why I'd like to acknowledge my editor friend, Joyce Gilmour, who won't let a missing comma or extra quotation mark get by her. You have a gift. Thanks for sharing it with me.

A special acknowledgement to the students of Accompsett Elementary School in Smithtown, New York, and the students of Brooklyn Elementary School in Brooklyn, Wisconsin, who were the first children to preview this manuscript. Thank you for your wonderful feedback and precious comments. Without all my Elliot Stone fans, including my own three children, this series would not have been possible.

And finally, I want to thank Francine Poppo Rich, and Blue Marlin Publications for believing in my work and bringing this project to fruition.

Thank you, all, for giving me a boost up the ladder of success. I couldn't have done it without you.

To Aunt Marie

For introducing me to Lake Bomoseen almost forty years ago, and for the priceless memories which led to the creation of this book.

— LP Chase

To my three sons, James, David, and Mark for keeping me young at heart.

— Carl DiRocco

CONTENTS

CHAPTER ONE
Off to Lake Bore-Me-to-Death

"A month? Are you kidding me, Mom? What happened to one-week vacations?"

"I thought you loved Lake Bomoseen, Elliot," she said, rolling another suitcase toward the front door.

"Yeah but—?" I followed behind my mother like a puppy. "You know how much fun Cassie's parties are. Her parents are renting a blow-up jousting arena; they have a full basketball court in their backyard and an outside movie theater. Plus, they have an amazing pool. Practically every kid I know is going. Can't I just stay with Jake, and you guys go to Vermont? I'm not a little kid anymore. This is our graduation party!"

We were going into fifth grade, and that meant we

were moving to a new school.

No response. Mom kept packing like a robot on a mission. So I tried a new angle. "When am I going to see my friends?"

Still nothing.

Jake has been my best friend since kindergarten. And Cassie started hanging out with us in third grade when she helped us solve a major mystery. She's super smart. Now, we're like a trio. Whenever there's a problem to solve, the three of us do it together. Like peanut butter and jelly...and bread. She's the bread. She keeps it all together. I guess I'm the peanut butter because I stick with it, and Jake, he's definitely the jelly. He can be a mess sometimes.

"Do we have to stay for a whole entire month?" I blurted, as she passed by with more bags. "Besides," I threw in, "Lake Bomoseen is boring." I kept making up stuff as I went along. "There's nothing to do. It's just a dumb old lake." I REALLY wanted to go to that party.

The woman did not budge. Instead, she shot me a glare and dropped a stack of pillows near the front door. "Something came up with Dad's job, and they need him to work with a client up there. Now stop whining. You'll have plenty of other parties, Elliot. And besides, you always have a ball in Vermont. It was never boring before."

Just then my little sister, Sam, ran into the room chanting relentlessly, "You're gonna miss the par-ty, you're gonna miss the par-ty."

I spun around like a top. "Shut up, Sam!"

"Elliot!" Mom blew her hair out of her eyes. "For someone who doesn't want to be treated like a little kid, you're certainly acting like one."

"But, Mom," I pleaded, trying to ignore the fact that I just told Sam to shut up and that my brat of a little sister was now sticking her tongue out at me. "It's not fair."

She handed me a suitcase. "You want fair? Start carrying this stuff out to the car."

I grabbed it from her and stormed out the door. Some vacation this was going to be!

CHAPTER TWO
Interesting Possibilities

I stared out the car window and daydreamed as we got further and further away from home. I couldn't believe I was going to miss the party of the century AND I wasn't going to get to hang out with Jake for a whole month. I was trapped in the car headed straight for Lake Bore-Me-to-Death.

Dad was driving, Mom was up front clicking through radio stations, and my sister Sam and I were in the back, separated by our baby brother's car seat. My mom always puts Tommy between us, like he's some invisible force field that will stop us from fighting. Yeah, like that'll ever happen!

"Illinois," I called out, for my mom to write down. We always play the license plate game on long car trips. And, of course, I always win.

"That's not fair!" Sammy looked up from making

one of those string bracelets. "Elliot's not giving me a chance." She went back to making more knots.

"Oh, stop it." Mom said. "There are plenty of states to go around."

Tommy looked right at Sam and made raspberry noises with his tongue. "Plbbbb."

I cracked up because his timing was perfect for an almost two-year-old! I gave him a baby high-five, and then got in trouble for teasing my sister. We're not supposed to gang up on her. But then I saw a new license plate, and my evil side got the best of me. I leaned across Tommy and got real close to Sam's ear, like I was going to tell her a secret, and hollered, "California!"

"Ahhh!" She jumped so high I thought she'd hit the roof of the car. That's when my mom's head whipped around. Daggers from her eyes shot over the headrest.

"Sorry, Mom," I said, wincing. I knew I'd reached my limit. Then Dad chimed in with some news that caught my attention.

"So, Elliot, did you catch any of that special I was watching last night?"

"Nah. Whatever it was, it seemed kind of boring."

Mom rolled her eyes. "That seems to be the word of the day."

"Aw, you should have watched it with me," Dad said. "It was on one of those history channels."

Oh brother. Dad and his educational channels – he could put you to sleep.

"Seriously, Elliot, you would have been intrigued. It was about the Loch Ness Monster."

"Wait. Loch Ness Monster? What's that?"

"See?" Dad got all proud of himself. "Loch Ness is the largest body of fresh water in Scotland."

Here we go.

"It's something like twenty-three miles long and almost two miles wide. Isn't that interesting?!"

"Oh, yeah, that's…that's real interesting." I rolled my eyes. "So? The monster part?"

"Well, for many years, people have been reporting sightings of a monster, or prehistoric-like creature swimming in the loch. They say it has a few humps and a long neck that juts out of the water."

Sammy cringed. "Stop talking about monsters. I don't like monsters."

"That's sick!" *Now this, I could get into.* "Did they show pictures?"

"Yeah. A few," Dad said. "Reports of sightings go as far back as the 1930s and as recently as only a few years ago. In fact," he continued, "there's lots of speculation as to whether or not these stories are real."

"Whoa." My brain was whirling. I wanted to see

pictures of this thing. "What did it look like, Dad? A giant swimming dinosaur? Where is it?" I leaned forward. "Do you think it's true?" I fired off questions without giving him a chance to answer. *Man, where was Jake when I needed him?* Then my mind made the connection. "Hey wait, Dad, did you say *fresh* water?"

"Uh huh," he nodded.

Sammy gasped. She turned white.

"So that means *LAKES* and stuff, right?" I blurted, before the Sammy-fest started. The wheels in my head clicked into overdrive. That's when my father's answer changed everything.

"Yep." He nodded at me through the rear view mirror. "That's what it means. Lakes and stuff." He emphasized my words. "They mentioned quite a few places where there have been sightings of sea monsters. But they don't call all of them the Loch Ness Monster. They have other names. Let's see, there were some in Canada, England, New York." He paused for a moment, glancing up at me through the rear view mirror. He raised his eyebrows. "And...even some parts of Vermont."

"GET OUT! VERMONT?" I shrieked, pulling myself right up to his seat. "You think there's one in Lake Bomoseen? How can we find out? This is awesome!" I was so psyched. I finally had a reason to actually *want* to be at that cabin. Maybe Lake Bore-Me-to-Death wouldn't be so boring after all.

By this point, Sam started crying, "I don't want a

monster in the lake."

"Waaa!" Tommy wailed now, too. "No monsa! No monsa!"

"Hubert!" Mom scolded, trying for a whisper. She turned to Sam and Tommy. "There are no monsters in the lake, sweeties. No monster, Tommy. I've been swimming in that lake all my life."

"No monsa?" Tommy asked me through a mouth full of juicy fingers. Man, he's so cute when he does that.

"No monsa," I said, mimicking him. He smiled.

Mom looked back at Dad and me with "The Eyes." You know them. The you-better-not say-another-word-about-this-or-you're-dead-meat eyes. Dad pretended to button his lip. "We can look it up later. I brought my laptop," he whispered with a wink, through the rear view mirror. I gave him a slick nod.

CHAPTER THREE
Almost to Fish Hook Lane

I knew we were almost there because the closer we got to the lake, the more it looked like Country Bumpkinville. Compared to home in New York, that is.

"Are we almost there yet?" whined Sammy. "I'm hungry."

"Shhh," my mother said, pointing back at Tommy, who was sleeping. "A few more minutes," she whispered.

Tommy's lips were puckered with a drip of drool

running down his chubby cheek. His little fingers grasped onto a piece of my shirt, but I didn't mind. I just stared out the window wondering about this sea monster thing and hoping that maybe this year we'd have some decent kids staying at the cabin next door. Usually, either the house is vacant, or there's some old lady always yelling at us.

As we drove around the lake, I noticed a lot of people. A bunch of kids were splashing each other in the water. Others were jumping off a yellow floating dock. There was even a floating slide. A few boats passed by, making ripples in the water.

Sammy gasped. "Look at thaaaat." She pointed out the window. The sun threw wild orange reflections off the tips of the waves. I had to admit it looked really cool.

Finally, we made the famous turn on Lake Willow Road – the road that led to Myron's General Store. Myron's sells the best banana taffy and every single flavor soft-serve ice cream you can think of. The best part is that it's close enough to our cabin that I can ride my bike there. That is, as long as I'm with someone.

"There's Myron's!" Sammy shouted. "Can we go to Myron's?"

Mom shushed her again.

"Not yet, Sammy. Let's just get settled first," Dad told her. "We have a whole month here."

Just then, I saw a big crowd of people standing in line at the boat rental place. Right next to them was a guy in a little hut. The sign overhead read, *Soggy Joe's*.

"Hey Dad, what's he selling?" I asked.

Dad pointed out the window. "It's a used golf ball stand."

"Used? Who would buy used golf balls?"

He laughed. "People who stink at golf, like me. We don't want to spend a fortune on the expensive golf balls, so we buy used ones. Hey, maybe I'll take you golfing while we're here. You'll get to see firsthand how bad I really am."

"Whoa, hold me back!" I teased. "I can't wait to go golfing with an old geezer. That'll be a REAL treat." Mom laughed especially hard at that one.

"All right, Liz, it's not that funny," Dad said, giving her an elbow in the ribs.

As we drove around the edge of the lake past the golf course, Mom made a clucking sound. "It's a shame about that place. What they're doing."

Dad nodded in agreement. "Bill is hoping things will pick up. Hopefully, his new plan will buy some time."

"What?" I butted in. "Who's Bill? And what plan?"

Mom looked back at me. "Bill Melton, the manager of the golf course. The place hasn't been doing as well in the past few years as it used to, so the owner wants to close it down and sell the property."

"Oh." I shrugged my shoulders. *Whatever.*

"He runs the pro shop, too." Dad added.

I thought about it. "Wait. You mean the little store on the edge of the cliff that sells the giant candy bars at the counter?"

"That's the one."

Oh man, I thought. It would stink if that place closed. No more humongous chocolate bars for only 75 cents.

I looked up and realized we were driving into the woods. That meant we were almost at the cabin. I knew the directions by heart. Two blocks in and bear left on Fish Hook Lane. The old wooden sign, or what was left of it, was nailed to a tree and pointed up to the sky, but my dad knew which way to go. The sign's been that way forever.

The car bumped and rattled over the dirt road until we turned into the gravel driveway and continued up the hill to our cabin.

One thing that's really neat about the cabin is that the back is actually in the woods and the front is facing the lake. So it kind of feels like you're camping when you hang out in the back, and beaching it when you're in the front.

I felt a little excited about being here now. Not totally,

but a little. I couldn't wait to check out the water and investigate this whole sea monster phenomenon. *Maybe I actually will have a little fun here after all,* I thought, as the car crunched over the last of the gravel and slowed to a stop.

CHAPTER FOUR
The Arrival Surprisal

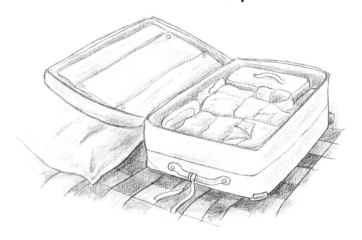

Sammy was the first one to jump out when Dad parked the car. I cleverly waited until everyone else got out. When the brains were dished out in my family, I got a double serving. I was in no hurry to start carrying a million things up the rocky hill to the cabin. Mom unbuckled Tommy, who was half awake and starting to cry, and took him inside. Dad opened the trunk and grabbed some bags. I just fiddled around in my seat, making myself look busy. "La…la la…la la."

"Elliot, can you give me a hand here?"

I winced. "Oh, man!" But I still took my sweet time getting out of the car. When I got around to the back, Dad handed me the fishing poles. "C'mon," he said. "Grab something else, will ya?"

I carefully executed my search through the trunk for

the lightest bag I could find. *Aha! Success.* The one with the potato chips in it. "Oh yeah. Snack time for Elliot," I sang.

Dad closed his eyes and shook his head. "I worry about you sometimes." Then he messed up my hair before heading inside. "C'mon."

Just then, Roxy, the neighbor's Springer Spaniel, came charging over to greet us like she always does, barking with lots of drippy slobber. She barks like crazy when a strange person or animal comes near the house. She pounced up on me, knocked the bag on the ground, and trampled all over my beautiful chips. "No! Not the chips!" I yelled. "Those were sour cream and onion! There goes snack time."

Roxy kept nudging me until I finally petted her. I patted her on the head because she's got those droopy jowls and I hate getting dog slobber on my hands. It's totally gross. But I guess she's sort of okay. She's growing on me. Sammy loves her, though. She ran over to Roxy and practically threw herself on top of the poor dog, kissing and hugging her. If the dog could talk, I bet she'd have been saying, "Blech! Get off me!"

Roxy wriggled her way out of Sammy's clutches and wandered back home. She usually just comes to say hello for a few minutes and then leaves again. She's like the neighborhood welcoming committee.

Right behind Roxy strolled Clarence, the neighbor's cat. He wandered over with a big attitude and a little smirk, weaving in and out of my legs as I picked up the flattened potato chip bag. Sometimes Clarence licks my ankles but it's not so bad. It tickles and feels scratchy like sandpaper – no huge amounts of slobber involved, so I can handle it. But this time, he actually stood there waiting for me to pet him with this snobby look, like, how dare I pet Roxy and not him. So I leaned over and scratched the fur on his back really hard like I always do. Clarence arched his back way up in the air like one of those Halloween cat pictures. I love when he does that. The best part is Sammy hates it. So I did it again. "Hey Sam, look at this," I yelled over to her. Being annoying is my specialty.

"ELLIOT!" she screamed.

Then I sprinted up to the house.

The wooden door squeaked open and slammed back with a crack as I bolted inside. I hadn't heard that slamming sound in a whole year. I hadn't even realized I'd missed it. *It smells like vacation in here,* I thought– that weird, woody, log cabin smell. Sammy was seconds behind me.

"Wait for me!" she shrieked, crashing into the door.

I gave it a quick push with my foot, just enough to open it for her, and then ran as fast as I could to my favorite bedroom.

We flew past Mom and Dad in the kitchen, our shoes clomping on the wood floors. "Whoa, you guys, slow down."

I ran into the first room on the left and dove on the bed. "I get this room," I called before Sam could claim it. I climbed up the ladder and scanned the room from the top bunk. I had forgotten how cool it was. Built into the walls were shelves filled with board games and decks of cards, and the windows looked out onto the lake.

"That's not fair," Sam whined. "You always get this room."

I was about to deliver a clever comeback, but then I noticed a gray suitcase on the lower bed. "Hey, what's that?" I knew it wasn't one of ours because our suitcases are blue and brown.

"Mom," I called out to the kitchen. "Did you put this suitcase in here?"

She peeked in the room. "What's that, Elliot?" she said with a weird grin. "Oh, *that* suitcase. No. Maybe someone left it here."

I scrunched my face. "That's kind of weird, isn't it?" I raised my left eyebrow to see if she'd fess up. I'd been working on that eyebrow move for some time now.

"Why don't you go bring those fishing poles down to the dock before you poke someone in the eye. I'll take care of the suitcase."

Oh well. I wasn't getting any info out of her. She's unbudgeable, if that's even a word. Jake would know. He's the word inventor. Instead, I took the poles and headed for the back door, which is technically the front door, even though we parked in the front, because the front door was really the back door. I know. It's confusing.

"Hey, Dad," I whispered on my way out to the screened-in porch. "Can we look up that stuff on the laptop when I get back in? You know, the Loch Ness Monster stuff?"

"A little later," he answered. "Let's get settled first."

I think that's Dad's favorite line, "Let's get settled first." He uses it for everything:

Hey, Dad, you wanna play chess? **Let's let our dinner settle first;** *Hey, Dad, wanna go for a bike ride?* **I just got in from work, let me get settled first;** *Hey, Dad, check this out.* **Just a minute. As soon as I get the bills settled.**

I walked out to the porch and let out a huffy groan. I was about to drop the fishing poles right there on the floor—it seemed like a good spot to me—until I heard a big, "Ahem!" I looked up and there he was again, watching me through the screen door.

I laughed out loud. "Alright. I'm going, I'm going." I hopped down the wooden steps, and headed for the dock.

As I looked toward the water, I could see two people standing there. *Who's that?* I wondered. It looked like a kid and a lady. The kid had binoculars. As I got closer, I almost flipped. It was a dead ringer for Jake. It couldn't be. "JAKE!" I shouted. "Is that you?" The kid pulled the binoculars away from his face and looked up. He started waving like a crazy lunatic. Holy cow! *It is Jake! And his mom!*

I hurried down to them, careful not to wipe out. I've done a few tuck-and-rolls down that hill in the past, and it's definitely not fun. Mrs. Weber planted a giant kiss on my cheek. I yanked my head as far back as I could. I didn't want her stiff hair to poke me in the face. I remembered the last incident when she nearly poked my eye out. *Man, she's gotta lighten up on that hairspray.*

"How are you, honey?" she said, rubbing my head.

"What are you guys doing here?" I asked. But actually, I didn't care *why* they were there. I was just glad they were. Jake put his fist up in the air, and I knew to give him a four-knuckle, high-five. That's our new, non-handshake, handshake.

"Well, we—"

"Surprise!" Mom shouted from the porch as she and Dad came down to meet us. "We invited Jake and Mrs. Weber to stay with us. I thought it would be good for you to have a friend around, since we were going to be here for so long."

"So THAT's why you didn't say anything in the house when I was throwing a hissy fit before? I'm really sorry about that, Mom."

"I know," she said. *She's alright.*

"Any time you need me to accompany you on vacation, I'll be happy to oblige," Jake said. Everyone laughed.

"This is great! Thanks, Mom." I gave her a big hug, and then she motioned with her chin over toward Dad. I knew exactly what she meant. "Oh, yeah. Thank you, too, Dad," I said. I'm getting better at picking up Mom's subtle hints.

For a split second I was hoping Cassie would spring out of the bushes and surprise us, too. I knew it wasn't possible because of her party and all. But still, I hoped. I waited. One second. Two seconds, five seconds. Aw, shucks. There were no more surprises.

"So how on earth did you keep this from me, Jake? You stink at keeping secrets."

"I know. I didn't find out until this morning."

"Good thinking," I said to his mother. "When did you get here?"

"Just a little while ago," she said.

"Nice cabin," Jake interrupted. This is gonna be awesome!"

"You're telling me! *Now* it's gonna be great! Too bad Cassie couldn't be here for this."

Jake's smile melted. "Yeah. That stinks. But hey, two out of three ain't bad."

I shrugged. "Yeah, I guess you're right."

"So," I asked Jake, as all the grownups went back toward the house, "whatcha looking at?"

Jake pointed across the water. "I was checking out that cool-looking island over there while I was waiting for you. Then I could have sworn I saw some weird black thing sticking out of the water. I tried to get a closer look, but the thing just rolled under the water and disappeared."

"Wait. What did you just say? Gimme those binoculars!"

CHAPTER FIVE
And Marley Makes Three

I snatched the binoculars from Jake's hands and adjusted the focus. I inspected the water. "Where? Where'd ya see it?"

Jake pointed toward the island across from us. "Over there. Why? What do you think it is?"

"Hold your horses." I looked through the binoculars and read PRIVATE PROPERTY. NO TRESPASSING. It was the sign on the bank of the island. Little waves crashed into the rocky edge. "I don't see anything."

"I'm not kidding, Elliot. It was black and stuck out of the water really far. And it was shaped kind of like a hook."

"This is so weird," I said to Jake. "My dad was just talking about some documentary on the Loch Ness Monster while we were in the car. He said there were sightings of sea monsters in other lakes too. Even in Vermont!"

"Get outta here!" Jake's eyebrows rose under his hat. "You don't think…?"

"I think we've got some investigating to do, Jakey boy!"

"Ooohhh!" Jake wailed, grabbing onto his hat with both hands. "Not again! How do I let you get me into these things?"

"Hey, at least we'll have something cool to do now."

"We can't investigate without Cassie. We need her for this," Jake moaned. "It has to be the three of us. She always figures out stuff."

"Yeah, I'm sure she'd rather be here instead of planning that awesome party *we're both* missing."

Jake snapped his fingers hard. "Darn. I keep forgetting about that."

"*I* sure didn't. Now, back to that island." I had to change the subject. "It's private property so we've never been allowed on it as long as we've been coming here. But maybe we can take the kayaks across to those rocks and set up a lookout point on the shore. You can almost see this whole side of the lake from there. We'll bring the binoculars and a camera and—"

"—And what?" Jake protested. "Sit there waiting for some make-believe stupid monster?"

"*Stupid* monster? Wait. What? Are you scared?" I pretended to bite off all my fingernails.

Jake kicked a pebble off the dock. "No. I'm not *scared*," he said, smirking.

"Okay. Here's the deal. My dad promised we could look up this stuff on his laptop later. So don't freak until we check it out first. Then if you want to, we'll investigate. Okay?"

Jake gave in. "Yeah. I guess."

"Alright, so don't go getting your boxers in a bunch," I said, flicking the rim of his baseball hat.

Just as I flicked, the hat flew off his head like it sprouted wings. "Hey!" Jake shouted, "My hat!" He leapt in the air to grab it and lost his footing. He fell backwards off the dock and smacked into the water, with a big girly scream. "Ahhhhh."

I was laughing so hard I could hardly breathe. I jumped in after him, and he started cracking up, too.

Jake wrang out the hat. "Man, this was *brand* new."

"Wait, shh, do you hear that?" I pointed up the hill.

"What?"

Muffled voices came from near the cabin next door. We heard car doors slamming shut, and the voices got louder.

Jake and I ducked our heads as low to the water as possible so we could spy. "Quick, underneath the dock," I ordered (nicely). "Nobody will see us here." Small waves slapped against the rocks every time a boat went by in the distance.

"Are there fish in this thing?" Jake's eyebrows furrowed.

I nudged him with my elbow and laughed. "It's a lake! What do you expect?!"

"But I can't see to the bottom. It's too dark. What if something bites me?"

My eyes bulged. "Nothing is gonna bite you. Shhh, they'll see us."

"So what? What are we even hiding for?" Jake asked.

Hmm. I wasn't really sure why. It was just fun. "I don't know. Just duck."

By now the voices were shouting. I noticed a girl running down the hill toward us. She looked about our age, maybe a little older. She was wearing an orange T-shirt with jean shorts and had long braid things. I'm not exactly an expert in girl hairstyles, but I think that's what you call them. It was hard to see with the sun setting right behind her, glaring in my eyes. She wasn't what you would call ugly or anything.

We watched her run straight toward the dock next to

ours with a baseball mitt in her hand. She wound that baby up like she was about to throw a Frisbee. Another little kid came running after her screaming, "Stop it! Stop it!"

Just when he caught up to her, she let the mitt go. "There!" she yelled back. "How do you like it, you little creep?!"

I think her plan backfired because the mitt plunked into the lake with a splash, completely drenching her.

"Uhh," she screamed. "This is all your fault, you little T-REX!"

"Grandma! GRANDMA!" the kid shrieked. He ran back up the hill to the cabin next to ours. *Great. Just my luck. Another little whining kid right next door.* Sammy was enough for me to deal with.

Jake burst out laughing, and the girl whipped her head to see where the laugh was coming from. She swung around so fast I thought one of those wet braids would smack her square in the face. She looked right at us.

"What's so funny?!" I think she was trying to sound mean, but her voice cracked. She wiped her face with her forearm. "Got a problem?"

"Great hiding spot," Jake ragged on me. I shoved him with my shoulder.

"Uh, no. We…uh, we're sorry." I turned to Jake. "Right?" He just shrugged.

"GOOD!" she snapped back. She huffed and headed back up the hill. I could hear her sniffling. I didn't know for sure, but I thought she was crying.

"Hey, wait," I called out. "What's your name?" But she never answered. "Nice going, Jake."

"Me? What did I do?"

"You're the one who laughed at her, dude."

"Well, it was kinda funny when she got soaked."

"I guess it was kind of funny. C'mon, let's go find that mitt before it gets ruined."

"And why do we want the mitt?" Jake made a face like he just ate a lemon. "Can't we just get out of this water? My clothes are getting heavy. I think I might sink."

I laughed at him. "I don't really *want* the mitt. I just want to get it is all." I swam out a bit. "Look, I think it landed over there."

"You're not gonna keep it, are you?" he called out.

I didn't even get to answer before Jake screamed, "Ahhh!" He freaked out, splashing like a mad man. "I think something just touched me!"

I kept looking for the mitt, swooshing the water around with my hands, ignoring his little scene. "No. I don't want to keep it. But if we find it, maybe we can get her to talk to us."

Jake swam as fast as he could (if you could call it swimming) toward the rowboat. It was more like a spastic splash fest. He hoisted himself up and flopped into the boat taking a few more exaggerated breaths. "Why do you wanna talk to her so bad?"

It was comical watching him try to stand up in the wobbly boat. "I don't," I said. "I was just—oh, here it is!" The mitt was floating just below the surface. I grabbed it and shook it out. "A couple more minutes and it would have sunk. C'mon, let's go put this on the porch."

I lifted myself onto the dock and offered him my hand. "Here, before you kill yourself." After I got him out of the rowboat, the two of us climbed over the rocks and onto the grass. Weeds and muck dragged from the bottoms of our sneakers, and water squished out with every spongy step.

"Eww, this is gross," Jake said, flopping himself onto the ground. "What is this slimy gack?"

"Ever hear of seaweed? Well, this is lakeweed."

Jake laughed. "Alright. Alright." He held out the ends of his wet shirt with his fingertips. "So when exactly does the fun start?"

We kicked off our waterlogged sneakers first, and then peeled off our socks.

"Boys, c'mon up. We're going to start barbequing now," Mom announced from the side window.

"Okay, we'll be right there." We picked up all our stuff and lugged it up the hill. As we neared the cabin, I heard music coming from the house next door.

"Hey, do you hear that Jake? Is that a guitar?"

"Sounds like it."

I threw my stuff back on the ground and crept toward the window where the music was coming from. Jake threw his hands in the air. "*Now* what are you doing?"

I waved him over. "Come here, Jake. You wanted fun...so here it is." I got down on my hands and knees and crawled up to the side of the house next door.

"What are you, crazy?" Jake's panicky whisper echoed against the open air. "I'm not coming over there!" His voice squeaked and crackled when he hit the high notes.

"Shhh." I climbed on a big rock, grabbed onto the windowsill and heaved myself up. There she was. The girl in the orange shirt. She was sitting on a bed, her hair all messed up and curly this time. And she wasn't crying anymore. I stared. That's when I realized I hadn't exhaled in a while, so I blew out some stale air. She was playing the guitar, looking down at the strings, all serious and stuff. For a second, I felt like I was watching a music video. She was really good, too. The more I watched her, the sweatier my palms got. My fingers started to burn. It was hard to hold on. Then Sammy came barreling out of our cabin.

"Elliot! What are you doing up there?" she shouted. "I'm telling."

Oh crud! Not now. I jerked my head to motion her inside. Luckily, Jake ushered her out of the danger zone. But when I turned to look back into the window, the girl was staring straight at me. I didn't move a muscle. I gulped.

"MARLEY!" she shouted, startling me right off the ledge and onto the ground.

"Ouch!" I rubbed my butt. My heart hammered out of my chest. I scrambled to my feet in a pathetic attempt to escape, but she was standing right at the windowsill, peering down at me. I froze.

"My name," she barked. "You wanted to know my name. It's Marley." And she slammed the shutters.

CHAPTER SIX
Orange Crush

Jake and I left everything on the grass and high-tailed it up the hill. What a rush! My heart rattled my ribcage. I wondered if the major adrenaline surge was because I got caught spying or because the orange shirt girl was totally cute. *Marley. Nice name.*

Jake ran ahead of me. "Hey, wait up. Did you hear her playing that guitar? She was pretty good, wasn't she?" I gasped for a few breaths and kept walking.

Jake leaned over to catch his breath. "If you say so. C'mon, those cheeseburgers are calling my name," he said, rubbing his stomach. "Can you smell that?"

"Are you even listening to me, Jake? She plays the guitar and her name's Marley." I looked back toward her window, and my stomach twisted in spaghetti knots. The shutters were open again, and I could see her peeking out at us.

Jake smirked. "Okay, so you got all the necessary info about mystery girl."

"She's looking at us right now," I said.

Jake turned to look. "Okay, loverbo—" he stopped dead in mid sentence.

"WHAT?!" I shouted.

"Elliot, LOOK AT THAT!" Jake's hand shook as he pointed out to the lake.

"What is it?" I turned to look. I shook my head to make sure I wasn't hallucinating. There was no need for binoculars this time.

Just beyond the house, a huge black creature-like thing rolled on the surface of the water. As we watched, its neck stuck out of the water, curled, and went back under with a ripple. We stood there frozen in silence. Waiting. Watching. It never came back up.

We dropped our jaws and bugged our eyes.

I choked the words out. "What was that thing?"

"Th-that's what I was talking about," he said. "What was it?"

I panicked. "Holy crud! That doesn't look like any fish I've ever seen. Where's the camera? We've got to get the camera!"

Jake stood still for a minute. Then he came to. "This is totally freaky, man."

"I know. We have to tell my dad. We've got to get on his laptop and find out what these sea monster things look like. We might be on to something," I said.

"Yeah..." Jake hesitated, "okay."

I smacked him lightly on the head. "C'mon. Don't you want to find out?"

"Ouch. Yeah. But you have to admit it is kind of creepy thinking there might be a sea monster living under the water. And I'm new to this whole lake experience."

"That's what makes it so cool."

"Well, I don't know about you," Jake said, his voice hitting the highest note I'd ever heard, "but this monster thing has me all worked up."

I patted him on the shoulder. "C'mon, let's get up there and tell my dad." I took off like a jackrabbit, leaving Jake in my dust. I'd just about reached the stairs leading to the screened-in porch when Jake caught up and shoved past me. "Last one upstairs is a loser!" he shouted over his shoulder.

I leaped up two stairs at a time trying to catch up to him. "Yeah, right." I buckled over laughing. "Like I'd ever let you beat me." We pounded the stairs like two geeky gorillas and barreled into the screened-in porch.

"DAD! DAD!" I called out. We pushed in the door to the cabin. Dad was sitting in the den.

"Whoa, back up you guys. What's the big rush? And take off those wet clothes and put them on the porch. Your mother will have a fit."

We stayed in the doorway to undress. "Dad, we just saw something in the lake. Something—"

"Huge!" Jake interrupted, gulping some air. "And I saw it before. Down at the dock. With the binoculars."

"It's definitely some kind of sea monster," I said, trying to convince Dad.

Sammy cried out from the doorway. "Daddy, you said there were no monsters here!"

Oh no. Not again. "We know what we saw!"

Dad hugged Sammy and shook his head at us. "It was nothing, honey. Don't you worry. Now go to the table. I think dinner is ready." He rubbed her shoulders and sent her on her way.

"But, DAD," I said, peeling off my wet shirt and chucking it onto the porch.

He put his finger up to his mouth motioning for us to hush. "Let's not get hysterical just yet," he whispered.

"Can we please look up that Loch Ness stuff now?" I asked. I could see he was about to make one of his excuses, so I begged. "PUH-LEASE?"

"You have to see it, Mr. S!" Jake said. "It's huge and definitely NOT a fish."

"Yeah?" Dad pondered. He tapped his hand on his chin. Jake and I stared at him and waited. That's when Dad got up and came over to the doorway. "Let me have a look," he said. He went onto the porch and looked out onto the water. "Where did you say you saw it?"

We followed him. "Right there." I pointed.

"And that's exactly where I saw it before." Jake showed Dad the spot near the island.

"You know what?" he said slowly. "Let's do that, after dinner."

"Thanks, Dad."

"But only on one condition," he added. "No mention of this at the dinner table. I don't want Sam and Tommy to have any more meltdowns."

Jake and I answered at the same time. "Deal!"

We inhaled our cheeseburgers and waited impatiently for Dad to finish talking with Mom and Mrs. Weber. *This could go on for hours.* I couldn't stand waiting any more. I thought I would burst. I had to get to the laptop and look up that sea monster stuff.

Finally, Dad excused us from the dinner table, and we followed him into the den. Tons of websites came up on the topic. There were pictures too, and they looked a lot like the thing we saw in the lake. They called the monster *Nessie*. And one site said they even opened a whole souvenir shop with stuffed sea monster toys, sweatshirts, and everything. One of the pictures looked exactly like what we had seen.

"Dad, look! This was it. Or something like it."

"Yeah," Jake said. "That's it."

Dad clicked more websites about the monster in Lake Champlain. "They called that one *Champ*," he said. Jake's eyes bugged out of his head.

Dad winked. "Maybe you two can find the Lake Bomoseen Monster," he said. "You want me to print this information?"

"You have a printer?" Jake asked.

"I have my portable printer in the car."

I pulled my fist down. "YES!"

Dad set up the printer and gave us all the info. He turned to Jake and me, placed his hands on both of our shoulders, and looked at us with this real serious face. "How about tomorrow," he paused, "we set out on a fishing expedition!" And he made those quote signs in the air when he said "fishing."

I knew exactly what he meant. We were actually going to look for this thing.

"I have a little work to do in the morning, so how about you guys fish off the dock first, and then we'll load up the boat for the afternoon? Sound good?"

"YES!" I looked over at Jake. I think all the color drained out of his face.

I patted him on the back. "It'll be okay, buddy." And then he pretended to faint.

CHAPTER SEVEN
The Bait Debate

I thought morning would never come. I was so excited about our potential sea monster that I think I woke up a million times that night. Then finally, the sun made an appearance through a crack in the blinds.

I hung upside down from the top bunk and shook Jake's bed. "Jake. Get up!"

He rubbed his eyes. "Huh?"

"C'mon. Let's get rolling."

Mom and Mrs. Weber were in the kitchen making breakfast. I could smell it from our room. Actually, Mrs. Weber was doing the cooking. That's her specialty. She has a catering business and people come from all over for her famous blueberry crumb muffins. They kind of remind me of my favorite cereal, Fruity Pebbles, with a thick layer of crumbs. Mmm.

"You boys are up bright and early," Mom said. "What are your plans for today?"

"Going fishing on the dock for a while. Then Dad's taking us out on the boat."

We each grabbed two amazing muffins and sucked down some orange juice. We waited for Dad so we could head out for some bait and Dad's fishing license.

"Want any eggs, boys?" Mrs. Weber asked, waving a spatula in the air.

"No thanks, Mrs. Weber," I said. What I really wanted was to take another muffin for later, but I didn't want to seem like a pig. Jake held up his plate. "I'll take some eggs." Of course he would. The kid was a bottomless pit, and he still weighed less than me. Go figure.

Dad came into the kitchen and poured a cup of coffee. "That Loch Ness stuff was pretty neat last night, wasn't it?"

Mom rolled her eyes.

"Yeah. So do you think something like that could be living in this lake?" I asked. "That would be awesome."

"There better not be," Jake protested. "You're not getting me in the water ever again if there's a sea monster lurking around, waiting for lunch."

Dad let out a deep, belly laugh. "I think you're safe for

now. There's probably not one in this lake. Even though this is the biggest lake in Vermont, it's probably kind of small for a sea monster. And even so, legends say they are harmless sea animals that live in the lake. Nothing to be afraid of. None of the ones that supposedly exist have ever harmed a human."

Jake's eyes widened. "Oh, I feel better now."

Dad laughed. "But seriously, getting back to the Loch Ness Monster, people have been debating its existence for years. You saw that in the research last night."

Jake made a fake gulp sound. "Uh huh."

"Oh, are you boys looking for a sea monster today?" Mrs. Weber teased. "Better eat up. You'll need all your strength."

"Trust me," I said. "If there's a sea monster, I'm going to find it."

"And you're not going to talk about it around Sammy, right?" Mom said.

"Right."

Jake picked up a fishing pole and tugged on the tip, bending it down slightly. "I hope these are strong enough."

I elbowed him, and he gave up a chuckle.

"Okay," Dad said. "Let's go get you kids the bait so I can get a little work done before we head out on the boat."

As we were leaving, Sammy came barreling into the kitchen with Tommy in tow. "Where's everybody going? I want to come."

Mom walked us to the door. "They're just going out for some bait and a fishing license for Daddy," she said. "Why don't you go make some more of your bracelets until they get back?"

"Perfect timing!" I told Dad as the door slammed behind us. "It was about to get real noisy in there."

He laughed. "That's for sure."

When we got back from the bait store, we went down to the water's edge. The sun was just rising over the island, and everything glowed orange. It was so quiet – all you could hear was an occasional loon cry or a distant boat making tiny waves ripple over the water. Every so often, the rowboat banged against the dock when a bigger boat went by.

"Which dock do you guys want to set up on?" Dad asked.

"We'll stay on the small dock right here," I said. We had two docks. One was shaped like a T and had the big boat tied to it. The smaller dock was closer to Marley's house. And that's where I wanted to be.

Dad put down all the rags and tackle box. Jake was still holding the poles.

I climbed up and set the two Styrofoam buckets filled with bait on the dock. Two dozen feisty little minnows.

Scratch that. Two dozen *clueless* little minnows.

I took the cover off and looked at the fish. "Do you know you're about to become lunch, little fellas?"

One minnow was already floating at the top while the others did crazy laps around the bucket. When I actually thought about it, it did seem a little barbaric. Sticking these poor unsuspecting fish on a hook, so they could be eaten by another fish. Gross. But, still fun.

Jake dropped the fishing poles and startled me. "I'm going to catch the biggest fish of the day!" He clapped his hands over his head and did a little swivel motion with his hips. "You just watch how skilled I am. Watch and learn."

Dad quietly set up the hooks on our fishing poles.

I let a tiny smile creep through my attempted stone face. "Are you planning to catch 'em with that slick dance maneuver? Impressive!"

"You've heard of doing a rain dance?" he said. "Well this is my new fish dance." He did it again. "It attracts the biggest fish."

"Is that so?" My dad finally chimed in with a chuckle. "You going for the sea monster, Jake?"

"No. No. No. I don't mean *that* big, Mr. S." Jake waved his hands in the air. "No way."

"Hey, last year I caught twelve fish in one morning," I chimed in.

"I'll bet you I still get the biggest catch of the day," Jake challenged me.

"You're on!"

"You guys all set?" Dad asked.

"We're good," Jake and I answered in stereo without even looking up.

"Okay, then. I'll be right there on the porch if you need me."

I picked up my fishing pole and was about to reach for the hook, when I heard something. "Shh." I stopped short. The fishing line swung past Jake's face missing his nose by a millimeter.

"Whoa. You almost hooked me," he said with a laugh.

"Shhh. You hear that?" It sounded like something splashing in the water. I felt a jolt of electricity zip through my legs.

"Hear what?" Jake asked, fiddling with his fishing pole.

I looked around. Then I saw two kids swimming a few houses down. "It was nothing," I said.

"Yeah, so. The minnows?" Jake got me back on track.

"Um," I stumbled. "Let's see. First, you get a minnow out of the bucket—"

"With my hands?" Jake's voice cracked. "Can't we

just use dough or something?"

"As I was saying," I continued. "You grab one of these little guys, and they wiggle a lot so don't drop 'em. Then you hold the hook like this and hook it through the top and out the other side. This way the minnow can still swim."

"Why does it need to swim? It's just food, right? Can't we sprinkle them on top of the water like goldfish flakes?"

"Uh...because they're called BAIT," I laughed. "And they're supposed to attract the big fishies," I said in a baby voice. I tried to make a joke, but the truth is, I really didn't know how to put a stupid minnow on a stupid hook either. Usually Dad did it. But I didn't want to be a wimp and go ask for help. And besides, I'm not a little kid anymore. I shouldn't have to ask my dad to bait my hook.

"All right, Mr. Minnow Man," Jake said. "You do the first one."

Great. "Okay." I had about as much confidence as a turtle. I wish I'd had a shell to back my head into. "Here goes."

I plunged my hand into the cloudy water and the minnows went crazy, flitting this way and that. "Fast little buggers," I said, grabbing and coming up empty. After about four tries, I finally did it. "Got one!" I shouted. "Wait. He slipped out of my fingers." Water was splashing, Jake was squealing, and I still had no bait. I tried again, and finally got hold of a big slippery one.

The minnow thrashed and flapped in my hand while I balanced the fishing pole between my knees and tried to get the hook through its back. Sweat dripped down the sides of my face. *This looked a lot easier than it really was.* Little by little, the minnow wriggled right out of my clutches and flopped onto Jake's sneaker. "Ahhhh!" he screamed and fell over like it was a grizzly bear attacking him and not a one-inch minnow. The fish did a few back flips until it fell between one of the planks on the dock and made a teensy splash in the water.

Jake looked up at me with a sinister smirk. "Ha, ha. How'd that work out?"

I held back a laugh. "Why don't you give it a try?" I motioned toward the bucket. "Well?"

Jake stretched his mouth into a tight line as he lowered his hand into the smelly fish water. He whimpered every time a minnow grazed his skin. "This is why we need Cassie. She'd probably have gloves and goggles and nose plugs."

"You're probably right."

We were both staring into the bucket when a voice startled us.

"You guys are such babies!"

"Huh!" Jake's fishing pole came crashing down.

"Uh, Marley. Um. Hi." I totally tripped over my words. My ticker picked up speed.

CHAPTER EIGHT
Jeff

I tried not to stare.

"Here, let me show you how to do this." Marley climbed onto the dock with us. Water splashed as she grabbed the bucket of minnows with a quiet huff. "Do you want me to bait both hooks?" The weird thing was she reminded me of Cassie, the way she just took charge. No nonsense.

She looked up waiting for an answer. "Well?"

I was torn between wanting her to help so she would stay there with us, and wanting her to leave so she wouldn't think I was a total loser. I opened my mouth but no sound came out.

"Yeah, sure," Jake finally answered for me. Thank goodness for best friends.

Her face relaxed. "I'm... I'm...sorry. About yesterday," she began. "I mean... I'm sorry I was so rude to you guys yesterday."

"Ah, don't worry about it." I waved my hand. "We were being jerks, anyway."

Jake gave me a look. "Speak for yourself."

I gave him a look right back.

"Truce?" she asked.

"Truce," we both agreed.

"So, what happened to make you so mad?" I asked her. I wasn't just trying to be nice. I really wanted to know.

"My little brother tossed my journal out the car window, and I think it went into the lake," she said. She looked right at me with her eyes wide open. That's when I noticed that they were totally green and sparkly.

I didn't want to sound clueless, but it was only a journal. *Couldn't she just start a new one?* I'm no journal expert, but it didn't seem like that big of a deal. Then Marley answered my next question before I even asked it.

"You see," she started. "There was this really important fax that came to my father last week."

"Here?" I asked, pointing up to the cabin next to mine.

"Yeah," she said. "I live with him and my grandmother."

"But wait," I said to Marley. "How come I never saw you here before?"

Jake hushed me. "Let her finish."

She looked down. "We lived on the other side of the lake, and this cabin was for my grandparents when they wanted to come spend time here. But now my parents are divorced."

Jake jumped in. "Mine too. Only I live with both. Some of the time with my mom and some with my dad."

Now I shushed Jake.

"So," she continued, "I'm not supposed to be in his office, and I definitely shouldn't have read the fax, but I did. It was about his job. It said something about if he doesn't make a profit this season, they are going to sell off the business and then he'd be out of a job. And something about working with someone on a financial plan."

"Wow. That can't be good," I said.

"No, it's not," Marley kept talking. "I was still reading it when I heard the front door slam. It was my father, and he was heading toward the office." Her face looked panicked.

"What did you do?" Jake asked.

"I freaked and tried to put it back," she said. "But he walked in on me. So I hid the fax behind my back and told him I was just grabbing some printer paper and left. I folded it up and stashed it in my journal until I could sneak it back to the fax machine later. Only, I totally forgot I had it. Next thing I knew, we were in the car coming back from dinner and my little brother, who's always causing trouble, started annoying me and we got into a huge fight. He grabbed my journal and as we got near the lake, he chucked it out the window. That's when I remembered the fax, and I went ballistic. And *that's* when you guys saw me throwing Tyler's mitt in the lake to get back at him."

I didn't know what to say. Then I finally broke the silence. "I have the mitt."

"You do?"

"Yeah. When you went inside yesterday, we found it and put it on the deck so it wouldn't get ruined."

"Thanks. I came out to look for it last night. I really didn't want Tyler to lose his mitt or get in trouble. And we both would have been in big trouble once my father found out."

"So what does your father do? I mean, like, where does he work?" I asked her.

"Right here," she said. "He runs the Paramount Point Golf Course and Pro Shop right on the lake."

"Wait a minute!" My one-watt brain made the connection. "Your father is Bill Melton?"

Jake gave me a confused look.

"The one and only, golf course guru," she said. "But not for long, if the business shuts down. I have to think of something to help him. I'm afraid if he loses his job at the golf course, then we'll have to move. We already had to sell our house on the east side of the lake. That's why we're staying in this house with my grandmother this summer."

"Hey, maybe Jake and I could help. Right Jake?"

"Yeah. Sure. It's safer than searching for a sea monster."

"Really? You will?—hey wait a minute." Her eyes flew open. "Did you just say sea monster?"

Just then, Sammy came running down the hill to the dock. "I wanna fish too. Wait for me!"

I shook my head. "Great! We can't tell you about the sea monster now. Sammy gets scared," I said, even though I was dying to tell her all about it.

"Oh, darn. So, you have a little barnacle, too?" Marley asked.

Jake giggled.

"You could call her that," I said. "She can be pretty annoying sometimes. Maybe we should introduce her to your brother."

"Yeah. Good idea." Marley picked up a minnow, grabbed the fishing line, and effortlessly slipped the hook right through the top of the fish. "My little T-Rex could use someone to play with." She handed me the pole. "Here you go."

"T-Rex?" Jake laughed. "I heard you call him that yesterday."

"Yeah, T-Rex, as in Tyler wrecks everything!" She laughed. I handed her Jake's pole, and she baited the hook for him, too.

Sammy came over and squeezed herself between us on the dock. If she got any closer, she would have been on my lap.

I tried to be a little patient. "Can you move over a little?" I asked bugging out my eyes.

She frowned at me and then looked up at Marley. "Hi. I'm Sammy. Look! I lost my tooth."

"Marley is baiting the hooks for us. You want one?" I tried to hurry her and get this over with.

Sam looked into the minnow bucket and swirled the water. "I like this one. He's cute. Wait. No. This one. Oh, look at the shiny one right here. He's my favorite. He looks like a Jeff. That's the one I want."

"You're naming a minnow?" I rolled my eyes. Even though I did think it was kind of cute in a funny sort of way.

"Jeff, it is!" Marley said. She swooped up the minnow and hooked him right through his back.

"What are you doing to Jeff?" Sammy shrieked in

shock. "You're hurting him!"

"No. Look," Marley said, trying to make her feel better. "You have to hook him like that so he can swim and attract the big fish. Watch."

Sammy made a face. "That's disgustipating."

"That's not even a word," I said.

Jake smiled. "I like the word. It actually fits. Disgustipating," he said again.

I rolled my eyes.

Marley cast the fishing line out into the lake. Sammy gasped. "I don't like him all hooked up like that."

"Shh," I said.

We all stared into the water, watching as Marley slowly cranked the reel. And we waited. Sammy looked on in horror. "It hurts him," she whispered loudly.

Soon we could see the shadow of a bigger fish lurking around the bait. I held my breath and leaned over the side of the dock to observe. Sammy peeked from behind us.

"Look, Sam," I whispered pointing to a big bass. "You're about to catch one right now."

Sammy lost it. "SWIM, JEFF, SWIM!" she screeched from the top of her lungs. We all jumped out of our skin, and the fish took off.

"Nice going!" I scolded. "You made us lose him."

Sammy folded her arms tightly. "I didn't want him to eat Jeff," she sniffed.

"Maybe fishing isn't for you," Marley offered. "You should go hang out with my brother, Tyler. He's about your age. Go on, he's up at the house." Then she looked at me and winked. My stomach sprang up to my throat and back down again.

Sammy looked up at Marley. "Okay, but first you have to set Jeff free."

I was getting frustrated. "It's just a stupid minnow!" I said.

"I guess it couldn't hurt," Marley said. She reeled the line back in, unhooked the minnow and tossed it in the water.

Sammy waved to the fish. "Bye, Jeff. Bye." Then she looked up at us. "Promise you won't hurt any more minnows?"

I nodded. I didn't say anything. I try not to lie, even to my sister.

"Eh, we'll try," Marley said. "Now go find Tyler."

Then I had a brainstorm. "Hey, Marley, since you're pretty good at this fishing stuff, do you want to come out on the boat with us? My dad's taking us a little later." Jake nodded like he thought it was a good idea, too.

"Oh, yeah. What's all this secretive sea monster

stuff?"

"It's a long story, but we saw a creature in the lake, and it looks just like pictures of the Loch Ness Monster."

She looked a micro-percent convinced. "The Loch Ness Monster? O-kay."

"Really," I said. "You'll see."

"Alright. I'm in. Let me just ask my grandmother. I'm sure it will be okay. And after that, maybe you guys can help me with…you know… the problem."

"Yeah, sure." *I love a good mission*, I thought.

"But you have to promise that you won't say a word to anyone." She put her hand out.

I put my hand on top of hers. It was soft, and for a split second I forgot what we were doing. Then Jake slapped his on top of mine. "Promise."

They both looked at me.

"Promise!"

CHAPTER NINE
Catch of the Day

I got on the boat fully prepared with my binoculars and my camera, hoping that we'd get a glimpse of that creature in the water. Jake had the snacks, and Marley had the sunscreen.

Dad drove us across the lake, past the big island into some of the coves. The boat hammered up and down on the waves, smacking the water as we picked up speed. It felt good when the wind whipped at my face, mixed with a spray of mist.

The whole drive out, I scanned the water for any sea monster sightings. I noticed some splashing and zeroed in on the surface, but it must've been a school of minnows because a giant sea gull swooped down and pecked something on top of the water. Every time I saw a splash or bubble in the water, my heart jumped.

We stopped the boat in a few different places to drop our lines, but nothing was biting.

My dad spoke over the noise of the motor. "We might have a better chance of finding your sea monster if we were actually catching some fish."

"How's that?" I asked.

"I'm thinking that it has to eat, right?" he said. "So the more fish there are in the area, the likelier it is that a bigger fish, or sea monster, would be drawn to that area."

It made sense. I guess. "So we better start catching something."

The sun was blazing hot, which meant the fish were hiding. We moved closer to the rocky edge because bass like dark places. They like to hide under the rocks, you know, in the murky parts. The only problem with getting too close to the rocks was that the hooks got jammed up on the slimy weeds.

Dad was pretty impressed with Marley's fishing skills. I think he expected her to be squeamish like other girls. She definitely wasn't like *other* girls.

"Where'd you learn how to bait a hook like that?" he asked her.

"My father," she said. "We fish all the time."

"That's nice," Dad answered. "You gotta teach these boys here. They need some help."

Marley laughed. "Yeah, I saw their talent earlier. Yikes!"

"Hey!" Jake shouted. "No picking on the weak and innocent."

While we took a break for some cheese curls and soda, I scanned the water again looking for any signs of a sea monster. There wasn't a single, suspicious-looking thing anywhere. I pulled out the binoculars for a closer look. Still, nothing. When we had finished our snacks, and it was obvious the fish weren't biting, Dad started up the boat. "Well guys, no sea monster today," he said. "Let's head back toward the cabin. We'll try one more spot on the other side of the island on our way back, but it doesn't look like we'll be catching much today."

Dad picked up speed, and the boat smacked the water again, sending showers over us. I leaned my head back. "Ahhh that feels good."

"So," Marley shouted over the noise, "still think there's a sea monster out there?"

"Yup. I do."

Jake perked up. "A giant sea serpent thingy is lurking in this lake, AS-WE-SPEAK," he said.

Marley winced. "You're sure about that?" I could tell

she didn't really believe us.

I jumped to Jake's defense. "It's true, Marley. I saw it with my own two eyes."

Jake chimed in. "I saw the thing twice. Once from the dock when I got here and again later, behind your cabin when Elliot was—"

"Eh-hem." I ended that sentence in a hurry–didn't need to rehash the climbing-up-the-window scene.

"Well anyway, we saw it. I swear."

Dad slowed the boat and circled for a perfect spot. Then he dropped the anchor one last time. The boat rocked gently and swayed to a stop. Marley baited our hooks again, and one by one, we cast our lines far out into the lake. And we waited. And waited. And waited.

"This is pointless." I pulled in my fishing line, and as I turned the reel crank, I got a tug. Then it started spinning by itself. Click, click, click, click. "Did you just see that?!" I looked up at Marley and Jake. I tried holding it still, but it turned faster and faster until it was buzzing like crazy.

"Elliot, stop," Dad called out. "You're probably tangled on something. Don't pull."

"I'm not! It's not!" I shouted. The line moved quickly toward the back of the boat. I tried to keep my balance as I followed where the line was going. "Help! I can't stop it."

"What is that?" Jake screamed.

Marley waved me over to her. "Give it to me! Give it to me!" she shouted. "You're probably just stuck like your dad said. You don't want it to get tangled around the propeller."

The clicking slowed down, and I managed to keep the pole still while I handed it over to Marley. Just as she took it, the line tightened. Then the pole bent like a horseshoe.

"WHOA! Elliot, what have you got on here?" she yelled.

The pole jerked so hard, it yanked out of Marley's hands and bounced onto the floor of the boat. The four of us were like a bunch of crazies. First, Jake leapt in the air, knocked the cheese curls off the boat, and practically landed in my dad's lap.

Marley shouted, "Get the pole! Get the pole!" Dad jumped up to grab it, and his hat flew into the lake. Marley dove onto the floor and landed square on top of the runaway pole. "Got it!" she shouted.

"Everyone, let's calm down," Dad said. "You probably have a pike on the line. They're pretty powerful fish, and they get big, too."

We stood up and tried to get control of the pole again. Dad helped Marley steady the line, but whatever it was started pulling on the line even harder than before. The reel was spinning like mad. Marley hopped around the boat with each tug. That's when Jake and I saw the ginormous shadow alongside the boat.

"DAD! DAD! Do you see that? JAKE, MARLEY, LOOK!"

Dad pursed his lips. "Humph," he said, like he was thinking something he wasn't ready to tell me yet.

Marley was speechless. Her knuckles were white from holding the fishing pole so tightly. The pulling suddenly stopped.

Jake sounded like a CD with a scratch in it. "I don't believe it. I don't believe it. I don't believe it." He was a mess.

From the angle we were at, the creature looked like it had a giant platypus face, but as the shadow moved further away from us, we saw a long serpent-like tail with a flipper at the end. It was as long as the boat. Maybe longer.

"Quick!" I yelled. "The camera!" I flipped open the seat cover and pulled it out. There was barely any time to focus, so I just snapped and snapped and snapped.

The pole jolted with a pop, ripped from Marley's hands and whipped her clear on her butt. The boat lifted in the air and smashed down on the water. We all screamed, even Dad, as we got drenched with water. It got eerily quiet. We waited in silence for what would come next. Then the fishing pole went limp. Jake and Marley both looked over at me.

I finally exhaled. "Holy crud! I just had a sea monster on my line!"

Dad checked the fishing line, and the hook was gone. The whole thing, bitten off. The creature was out of sight. I was waiting for Dad to freak out, but instead he looked at the three of us and shrugged. "Whatever it was, it's gone now."

CHAPTER TEN
Save the Minnows

We were all rehashing the events as Dad docked the boat in the slip in front of our cabin.

"That was the biggest thing I've ever seen," Jake said. He stretched his arms far apart. "The head was like this!"

Marley agreed. "What a rush that was."

"A rush?" Jake disagreed. "It freaked me out. I'm never swimming in that water again."

Marley giggled at him.

"Now do you believe me?" I said.

"You know guys, I still think it could have been a Northern Pike. What you saw in the water was a shadow. Sometimes your eyes can play tricks on you." Of course my dad had to be all logical and stuff. "You know how you can see shapes in the clouds? It's the same thing."

Is he nuts? I thought. *There's no way my eyes were playing tricks on me.* "Maybe, Dad, but I seriously doubt it."

Marley reached for the camera. "Did you get a good picture, Elliot? I'll bet the proof is right in here."

"I don't know. I snapped a bunch. Let's look."

I moved closer to her so I could see the viewer on the camera. I watched as she clicked through the pictures. Her hair smelled like a watermelon Jolly Rancher.

"This one is too blurry. No, not this one either." We kept searching for a good one. Most of them were a waste, but two came out clear enough to make out the image.

"LOOK!" She slapped her hand on my knee. "Here it is. Proof. We have proof."

I grabbed the camera from her hand and waved it in front of my dad. "*Now* tell me our eyes are playing tricks on us, all our eyes *AND* the camera all playing the same tricks? I don't think so."

Dad raised his eyebrows and nodded. "It definitely

raises questions." He turned off the motor and I jumped out first to help him secure the rope to the dock. When the boat was steady, my dad helped Jake climb off, and of course, I was the only one left to help Marley, and that meant she had to hold my hand. *Woohoo.* I smelled my palm first to make sure it didn't smell like rotten minnows.

"Thanks, Mr. Stone," Marley said as she got out of the boat. Then she eyeballed Jake and me. "That was unbelievable. I've never seen anything like that in the lake. Ever! Remind me not to doubt you guys again."

"See? I do not lie about serious things like sea monsters," Jake said.

"Now don't forget," she whispered so my dad couldn't hear. "You said you would take a ride up to Myron's with me later to search for the journal."

"Yeah, sure," I said. I wasn't about to blow a chance to hang out with Marley.

"You too, Jake?"

"I'm there! You don't have to ask me twice. Hello, banana fudge swirl."

"You can always bribe Jake with food." I patted his belly. "You better watch it, buddy."

"Ouch!" He gave me a shove. "That's hurtful."

"You guys are so mean to each other," Marley said with a smile.

71

I laughed. "Ah, he knows I'm kidding. That's what guys do."

"Seriously though, we'll go, say in an hour?" she asked.

"Yeah." I looked at my watch. "Meet you out front with the bikes in one hour."

"If we don't get eaten by the sea monster before then," Jake said.

"EH HEM!" It was Dad. He was holding all the fishing stuff: the poles, the bait, tackle box, and the towels. We could barely see him underneath all that. "Is anybody going to help me out here?"

"Oh. Sorry, Dad." We laughed and each grabbed something before heading up to the house.

As we walked up the hill, we could see a bunch of people at the front of the house by the driveway. Kids on bikes, parents. It was a mob scene.

"What the heck is going on up there?" I said.

Once we were closer, we could see it was Tyler and Sammy. They had a big table set up, and they were selling Sammy's string bracelets and lemonade.

"What's this?" Marley asked.

At the same time, Tyler and Sammy pointed. "Read our sign," they said.

SAVE THE MINNOWS was written in marker on

a sign taped to the front of the table. On the sign, they had drawn a cartoon picture of a fish caught on a hook. The fish was making a choking face with its tongue sticking out, and the fins were holding onto its neck. On the bottom it read, **IN MEMORY OF JEFF (who almost got eaten). PLEASE SAVE THE MINNOWS.**

"Nice drawing," I said pointing to the sign. "And by the way, fish don't have tongues."

"Go away, Elliot," Sammy said. "We have customers." She took a dollar from a girl and handed her a bracelet. Then she shoved the dollar bill into a jar, which was full of money. Holy cow! I couldn't believe she had made and sold all those bracelets. She's always walking around with string, but I didn't think she actually finished anything. And they were really nice.

"You seriously think you can save all the minnows?" I asked her.

"Yes!"

"How do you figure?" I laughed and looked at Jake and Marley. "Do you believe this stuff?"

"You'll see, Mr. Smartipantsicle," Sammy said.

"That's not even a word," I said, knowing full well it would get her all fired up.

"I'm gonna tell on you," she shouted.

I just ignored her. Not worth getting into trouble. And besides, we were thirsty, and on Tyler's half of the table was lemonade for fifty cents a cup. Sammy's beaded friendship bracelets were a buck. I eyeballed the one with orange beads because it matched Marley's shirt from the other day.

"Hey, Tyler, can I have a cup of lemonade?" Marley asked.

"Nope. Not unless you have fifty cents."

"C'mon. Just give me a cup. We just came from the boat so I don't have any money. I'll pay you later."

"Sorry," he sang. "No money, no drinkey." He gave Sammy a high-five.

"Ugh. You are such a brat!" Marley huffed.

I rolled my eyes. "It's no use. Let's go put all this fishing stuff away and go on that bike ride."

"We have to have lunch first," Jake said. "I need nourishment. Just in case I have to fight off any more beasts."

"Yeah, because you fought off that last one really good," I teased. Marley laughed and slapped her thigh.

Then Jake's mom pulled up in the driveway and got out of the car with two buckets of minnows. Tyler and Sammy ran over to her and each grabbed a bucket.

"What are you doing?" Jake asked his mom.

"The kids are earning money for a good cause. Isn't that cute? I ran up to the bait shop and got some minnows with their money."

Jake shook his head. "Wait a minute. That makes no sense. I thought they wanted to save the minnows."

"Duh. We are," Tyler mocked Jake.

"We're setting them FREE!" Sammy declared.

Jake shook his head. "Am I getting dissed by first graders?"

"I told you he was a T-Rex," Marley said, laughing.

We watched as Mrs. Weber took them and their minnows down to the dock. They emptied the buckets over the top of the water and actually waved goodbye to the bait.

When they finally came back I wanted to say, *You do know that they're still going to get eaten by the bigger fish?* But I just didn't have the heart. It would kill her. Sammy actually cared about these little fish.

"See?" Sammy smiled. "We're saving all the minnows. Even if we have to buy up every last one and set it free."

"Okay," I said. "Good luck with that."

Then a light bulb went on in my head, and I remembered what my dad had said on the boat earlier about the bait attracting fish. *If they keep dumping buckets of bait off of our dock, it's going to attract tons of fish. And they'll attract bigger fish...and...maybe even the sea monster.*

I think Jake and Marley thought the same exact thing because right when it hit me, they both looked up.

"This dock is going to be very busy at dusk," Marley said. "We better dust off the big poles."

CHAPTER ELEVEN
The Bike Trip

After lunch, Jake and I raced up the hill and wheeled our bikes from the shed. Dad came out of the house dressed in a suit and tie and was carrying a briefcase.

"Where are you going?" I asked him, lifting one leg over my seat. "It's vacation."

"I have to go see a client. Remember, this is a working vacation for me?"

"That stinks," Jake said. "I'd protest."

Dad laughed. "Yeah, I wish I could protest, kiddo, but this is a very important deal. If it doesn't end successfully, it could mean our regional office closes. Permanently. And I'd like to keep my job. So, sometimes, you have to make a sacrifice."

"Glad I don't have to work," I said, putting in my two cents. "Work messes up everything. Try to have fun, anyway."

Jake and I rode around to the front of the house to wait for Marley. Sammy and Tyler were still out front at their sales table. I couldn't believe they still had people coming to buy their stuff. Then I saw the friendship bracelet with the orange beads again sitting at the edge of the table. It was kind of cool. I couldn't believe my sister actually made it. I slowly rolled my bike closer to the table. Then, I checked my pocket to see if I had money.

Jake looked suspicious. "What are you doing?"

"Nothing. I'm…uh…seeing if I have enough money in case we get ice cream at Myrons."

"Oh! Okay," Jake said, exaggerating the "o's." "Right."

"Hey, we have to bring the camera with us. Want to go get it?" I said, changing the subject. "We should have it with us all the time. In case of sightings."

Jake laid his bike down on the ground. "I'll get it, but first admit that you want to take pictures of Marrr-leyyy."

I kicked some gravel up at him with my sneaker. "Quit it, Jake." I felt myself blushing.

"Ahh." Jake hopped in the air like he was jumping an invisible hurdle. "Okay, okay. I'll stop."

Sammy was busy pretending to be a grownup, selling bracelets to some kids from a few houses down. I touched the orange bracelet. "So how are sales going?" I tried to sound casual.

"Wouldn't you like to know!" she sassed at me. Then Tyler unleashed a devilish grin. *What was he, her sidekick now?*

"Fine!" I said, faking being insulted. "I was trying to be nice." Then I secretly slid the bracelet off the table into the palm of my hand. I didn't really want to steal it because stealing was wrong. But I didn't want her to know I was buying one either. That's all I would have needed with her big mouth. She'd tell everyone I was buying it for a girl. "Here!" I said, flipping a dollar in the air. It fluttered down in front of Sammy.

"What's that for?" she asked.

"Consider it my donation to your *Save the Minnows* campaign. Don't say I never did anything nice for you." *Phew.* I felt better knowing that I paid for the bracelet. Then, when she and Tyler weren't looking, I shoved it in my front pocket.

Sammy studied my face. "Are you up to something?"

"Nope," I said. "Now drop it."

"You are so petilliating, Elliot Stone!" she said.

"Petilliating?" I repeated. "Sam, that's not even a—"

Jake was running back with the camera. He burst out laughing. "That's a great one. Petilliating. What's that, like frustrating?" he asked Sam.

"Exactly."

I shook my head.

"What?!" Jake defended himself. "It's a good word. What about you? You say ginormous."

"That's different. Ginormous is like a real word," I said, glancing up at Marley's house to see if she was coming yet.

Jake gestured to my hip pocket. He must have seen me stuffing the bracelet in there. "Whatcha got in there, buddy? Huh? Huh?"

Roxy started in with the barking again, followed by the sound of gravel crunching. *Saved by the dog.* I parachuted right out of that conversation and left Jake hanging up there. The sound was Marley riding up the driveway. I pedaled toward her.

"Where were you?" I said.

"I was just taking a spin while I was waiting for you. You guys ready?" she asked.

"Yup." I looked back at Jake. "You ready?"

"Ready as I'll ever be."

The wind whipped at my face as we rode our bikes

down Fishhook Lane and headed to Lake Willow Road. I love that whooshing sound you get in your ears when you ride super fast. It must be how dogs feel when they hang their heads out the car window.

I was so lost in thought that I sped up past Jake and Marley. The conversation with my dad slowly crept up and nagged at me. *Lose his job?* I had never actually thought about that. *Could he really lose his job? Would we have to sell our cabin like Marley did? What about our regular house? Would we have to move?* It was all building like the pressure in a volcano. I was about to spurt out molten lava. I shook my head to get the thoughts out. *Nah. That's not gonna happen.*

Marley caught up to me. "Elliot, you okay? You seem like you're somewhere else."

"Yeah. I'm fine," I lied. I tried to focus on good things. Like cookie dough nacho ice cream at Myron's.

We were almost up to the boat rental place. You could see the golf course across the lake, and Myron's was coming up soon.

"Slow down, guys," Marley said. "We're getting close. See that boat ramp over there, and the sandy beach right next to it? I think we were around there when Tyler threw my journal out the window. It landed near those wildflowers."

I noticed people waiting in line at the rental place again, and other people dragging kayaks into the water from the ramp. I pointed to Soggy Joe's. "Hey, there's that used golf ball place."

"What'd you say?" Jake asked.

"Oh, it's nothing. My dad was just telling me about used golf balls."

Marley and I hopped off our bikes. "Let's check out over here, Jake," I said, but when I looked up, he wasn't behind me. I looked around. "Jake? Where'd he go?"

We looked back. "There he is," Marley said waving. "Jake! Over here!" He was still across the street balancing his bike and looking through the binoculars.

"What's going on?" I called out. "You see something?"

Jake lowered the binoculars and frantically gestured for us to come back. We threw our bikes on the grass and ran across again.

"You're not going to believe this," he said, "but I think I just saw the sea monster!" He pointed across the lake. "And it's right over there by the golf course. Keep looking under the cliff and watch the water." He handed me the binoculars. I held them against my eyes and slowly scanned the lake, adjusting the view until it was crystal clear.

"Where?" Marley demanded. "Show me!"

Just then, I caught a glimpse of something. It flapped the water surface and splashed back down.

Marley grabbed my arm. "DID YOU SEE THAT?" she shouted. "I just did!"

"I was about to. I lost my focus when you pushed me."

"LOOK!" Jake screamed. "It's over there now!" He pointed a little to the left that time.

"I can't see through these things. I have to refocus!" I fumbled with the binoculars. By the time I found the spot on the water, there was nothing but bubbles. "Jake, pull out the camera and get it ready," I shouted.

I could sense that the sea monster was coming up again. I think Jake and Marley did, too. We stood perfectly still—so still, you could hear the three of us breathing.

My heart short-circuited. I put my hand on my chest and felt it. "Can you guys hear that?" I asked.

"Hear what?"

"Never mind." At this point, I was sure I was losing my mind, and that was the next thing we were going to have to look for.

I sucked in a huge breath and focused on the water. Jake whispered to me. "You see it yet?"

Then, just as I expected, it returned. A narrow black neck stuck out of the water little by little until it was up about four feet high. It had a tan beak thingy at the end of its head. Then a big hump rolled in the water.

Marley screamed, "There it is!"

"SNAP NOW!" I yelled to Jake.

He snapped like a crazy man. "Crud! You scared me. You made me shake. Now the pictures will be messed up." Another hump rolled on the surface, followed by the tail and flippers.

I freaked. "IT'S STILL THERE!!!" But it rolled, then bubbled below the surface and disappeared. I couldn't take my eyes off the spot.

"Did you see that?" I shrieked. "Holy cow!"

"Do you think anyone else is seeing this?" Marley asked.

"I was thinking the same thing," I said. "But, it goes back under really fast, so maybe people actually miss it. I mean... I sort of came here hoping for a sea monster, so I was ready for it. You know?"

"Yeah, you're probably right," Marley said.

"Do you think it was the thing we almost caught on the boat this morning?" Jake asked.

Marley nodded. "It had to be."

"This is insane." I half-laughed and felt like I needed to pinch myself to make sure it wasn't a dream. "It can't be happening." *We have our very own sea monster?* I thought. *No way!*

The three of us huddled close as Jake clicked through some of the pictures, but most of them weren't usable.

"Nice going, Jake, I said. "Better not quit your day job."

"You try taking pictures with two psychos screaming at you," he said.

Marley giggled.

"Let me have this," I said, yanking the camera from Jake's hand. I continued clicking through the photos. Then we saw one. "Wait a minute!" I shouted. Jake had gotten ONE perfectly clear picture of the sea monster. One that clearly captured something jutting out of the water, and it most definitely was *not* a fish.

CHAPTER TWELVE
Coming Up Empty

And to think I was actually worried that this vacation might be boring. I'd been here less than a week, and it was anything BUT.

I still couldn't believe what was going on. Every sighting made me more curious. And nervous. I wanted to know what it was, but at the same time, I didn't. Especially when it had been on my fishing hook only a few hours before.

The three of us watched the lake a while longer. And, other than a boat going by or an occasional screaming kid jumping off a dock, there were no signs of that creature. At that point, it was kind of hard to focus on looking for a journal when there was possibly a sea monster making guest appearances at our vacation spot. I wondered if those kids would be swimming there if they knew what we knew. I wondered if I should warn them. *Nah. It's a harmless sea animal, like Dad said.*

But we promised Marley we would help her find the journal. And so we did. And then afterward, we would hit Myron's for some incredible ice cream before heading back to the cabin.

"Over here," Marley said, directing us.

We trampled a footpath through the wildflowers on the edge of the lake and searched for the missing book. I kept checking the water every few seconds to see if the sea monster had come back.

"Okay, guys," Marley said, "the journal is about this big, and it's—"

"Let me guess," I interrupted. "It's orange."

"How did you know that?"

"You wear orange a lot," I said, half-smiling.

Jake was behind Marley, making all sorts of gestures and kissing his hand like one of those kisses you'd see in the movies.

I looked right in his eyes and sent him a non-verbal message. He wasn't getting it. Then I gestured for him to zipper his lips so he'd get the hint to shut up. I totally didn't need any embarrassing scenes now. He knew exactly what I meant that time and surrendered with both hands up.

Marley looked behind her. "What are you guys up to?"

"Nothing. I'm just gonna have to kick Jake's butt later," I laughed.

"Oooh, I'm shaking in my boots."

"C'mon. Seriously, guys. You promised you'd help me find it. Keep looking."

Jake scratched his head. "I don't know about you two, but I can't concentrate. That sea monster might pop up and grab one of us." He monitored the water.

He was right. It was difficult to concentrate. I swatted at more weeds or wildflowers, or whatever they're called. I was hoping to find the journal and get the heck out of there so we could get back to more important things. Like the sea monster.

Jake became the official observation tower, and Marley was now crawling around on her hands and knees. I followed behind her.

"You said you wanted to help your dad, right?" I asked Marley.

"I have to," she answered with a slight sniffle.

"So, then we have to figure out how to get more people to go to the golf course. Why don't we try to come up with some ideas that will bring people here to the lake?" I suggested. "Getting him more business will help your dad better than finding the fax will. Right?"

"I guess so," she said.

Jake put down the binoculars and scratched his cheek. "How do you get more people to want to golf? Isn't golf like the most boring sport in the world? Besides bowling, that is," he laughed. "Maybe we should think about food. Good food will get more people here." He avoided crushing some daisies.

"Doesn't your mother feed you?" I loved to bust Jakes's shoes. Although, he did have a point. *People might like to have some food after they play golf.* "You know what? You might be on to something," I said.

Marley stood up and brushed the sand off her knees. "I know. What if we raise money to fix up the place?" she suggested. "You know, so my father can make the pro shop and the snack bar even better. Maybe add a game room and cool things like that."

"How are we supposed to raise that kind of money?" Jake asked.

"Think about it," Marley said. "If Sammy and Tyler could come up with a plan to make money, then we sure can."

I kept looking out into the water, distracted by every little ripple. I needed to chill out a bit and focus on something else. "Let's go to Myron's and write down these ideas. Then we can figure out how to make them work."

Marley was upset that we hadn't found her journal, but she agreed. We traced our steps back over the path until we reached our starting point by the boat ramp.

As I bent down to grab my bike, I caught a glimpse of something orange stuck in a bunch of cattails on the right side of the ramp. "Hey, look." I dropped the bike and ran to take a closer look. Whatever it was, it was jammed between bunches of stems. I had to work my fingers through and yank really hard to get it untangled. Finally, I pulled it out. It was a journal all right—*the* journal! And it was soaked all the way through.

Marley came running over and threw her arms around me with a great big hug. "You found it!"

I thought I would faint right then and there. I felt like the hero in an action film who wins the girl at the end. Only we weren't at the end, and all I did was find a little book. Even so, I enjoyed breathing in her watermelon shampoo. One thing was for sure… I didn't dare look up at Jake. This was enough blackmail material to last him a lifetime.

She let go of me, and I handed her the book. "I brought the key," she said, feeling around her back pocket. She pulled out a tiny silver key and put it in the lock giving it a gentle turn. The key stalled halfway around. She jiggled it a few times. She tried again, this time pulling on the top until it finally clicked.

Marley opened the journal and tried to fan the wet, stuck pages until she got to the back. Her shoulders slumped. "It's not here. The letter. It's not in here."

"I'm sorry," I said. What else could you say when someone loses an important letter telling her father he might lose his job?

Jake and I looked at each other with no clue what

to do next. I didn't have any superhero answers up my sleeve. No clever comments. No nothing. Marley frantically flipped through the pages, back to front to back. Most of the ink looked like it was faded and running off the pages from being in the water.

She looked up at us, with her eyes about to gush. "Now what?"

CHAPTER THIRTEEN
The Twist at Myron's

We hurried across to Myron's. Jake and I tried to convince Marley not to worry about the letter. "We'll come up with something," I promised, as the waitress came over to take our orders. I got the usual. Cookie dough nacho ice cream, with peanut butter sauce and hot fudge.

"Check this out," Jake pointed to the menu. "They have party cake dough and banana fudge chunk. I'll have both. Half and half." He smiled a big smile.

Marley sighed. "I don't know what to get." She slammed the menu closed. "I guess I'll just get the usual, strawberry crème twist."

When the waitress left, we continued swapping ideas. I remembered that every year since I'd been coming to the cabin, the Main House (an old hotel next to the golf course) held a summer dance. I remembered it because my parents always made me wear a suit, which I actually didn't mind, because it felt kind of cool to be all decked out.

"Did you ever go to the Main House Summer Dance?" I asked Marley.

"Yeah," she said, sort of matter of fact, like, *doesn't everybody?*

"Me too. I can't believe I never saw you there before."

The waitress brought over our ice cream and dropped a stack of napkins in the middle of the table with the check.

Jake dug right in. "Mmm. Mmm."

"So, back to the dance," I persisted. "What if we do something at the dance to raise money?" I suggested handing out flyers to save the golf course, or asking people for donations. I even resorted to thinking we could ask Sammy to teach us how to make those bracelets and we could sell those at the dance. "What about that?" I asked.

Marley looked hopeful. "I love those bracelets," she said, plucking a giant strawberry out of her ice cream and tucking it in her napkin. "But I don't know how to make them, and I'm not sure how much money that will actually bring us."

I pulled the orange bracelet out of my pocket and put it on the table. "Here's one that we could try to duplicate."

A sinister grin crept through Jake's lips, and I gave him a swift kick in the ankle.

"When did you get this?" Marley asked me.

"I uh, borrowed it to have as a sample," I said.

Marley put it on. "This is so pretty," she said. "But I'm not sure this is going to do the trick. I mean, it was okay to make a few bucks for the little kids, but we would need some serious cash." She picked another strawberry out of her bowl and smeared it on the napkin.

"What are you doing?" Jake pointed to the pile of strawberries next to her dish. "I thought you loved strawberry ice cream."

"I do, but I hate the big chunks of strawberries because the ice cream melts in your mouth, and then you're left with a big hunk of stuff on your tongue. It's gross."

"I will never figure out girls," he said.

We finished up our ice cream and talked some more about how we could help Marley's father.

"So, Marley," Jake said, "Elliot says you play a mean guitar."

She smiled so big I could see all of her teeth. "I'm taking lessons," she said. "I want to be a professional singer someday."

That sparked an idea. "Hey, why don't you play at the dance?" I said. "Maybe we could make some good

94

money that way!"

"Elliot, you're a genius!" She jumped up out of her chair. "That's a great idea. We could ask my father to talk to the coordinator and set us up as entertainment."

"What do you mean 'us'?" Jake said with panic in his eyes. "There's not a musical bone in my body."

"C'mon, Jake, it might be a good idea," I said. "We have the keyboard in the cabin. It practically plays itself." It was weak, but still it was an idea. "We could easily play background music."

"Do we even have enough time?" he asked. "When is this dance, anyway?"

"Good question," I said. "I think there's only three weeks left. It's usually at the end of July or early August."

Deep down, I didn't think we could pull something like that off. I mean, Marley was good at guitar, but it's not like we were an actual band or anything. Marley wrote some notes on a clean napkin, and we kept adding to the list.

Our brainstorming session was just warming up, and then my whole reason for wanting to help Marley changed. Big time.

Myron's has some tables outside in the back. I was only half paying attention when I caught a glimpse of two men coming out of the back room. One man went up to the register, and the other man came toward our table.

"Marley," the man said. "What are you doing here?"

"Um. Hi, Dad," Marley said. "These are my friends, Elliot and Jake. They're staying in the house next to Grandma's."

He extended his hand to me. "Nice to meet you. You must be Hubert Stone's boy."

My ears stood at attention as I shook his hand. *How does he know my father?* I must've looked completely shocked because Jake reached over and closed my mouth for me.

"Oh, maybe I'm mistaken."

"You're not mistaken," said a familiar voice from behind me. It was the other man at the register.

"DAD?! What are you doing here?"

"I told you I was having a meeting. Bill Melton is my client, and we came here for a bite when we were through."

My head did calculations like an electric adding machine. And before I could say anything, Marley blurted a confession to her father.

"Dad, I'm really sorry. I shouldn't have been in there. And now it's lost. I had the fax, and I meant to give it back—"

"Slow down. Slow down. What are you talking about?"

"Remember the other day when I was in your office? Well, I wasn't getting a piece of paper. Well I was, but then a fax came in for you, and I read it. And I didn't mean to read it. But I did. And it was about the golf course, and it was saying that if you didn't have a good season, that it would be shut down."

"You mean this?" He pulled out a folded piece of paper.

Marley was stunned. "Where did you find that? I was afraid you would get mad at me, so I put the fax in my journal but then I lost the journal and we just found it and it wasn't there—"

"Slow down, Marley."

"But, Dad," she said.

"Hold on a minute, sweetie." Mr. Melton rubbed her shoulders. "Marley, take a breath for a minute. I know about the letter."

"But, I…but…you do?"

"Yes. First of all, I found it folded under the back seat in the car so it must've fallen out of your journal. But I knew the business was in trouble, anyway. That's why Mr. Stone is here. The fax was from him."

Well my ears certainly perked up at that point. Like a dog that hears the neighbor's cat prowling in the bushes, I was ready to defend. *What does my father have to do with this?*

"What?" She shook her head. "I don't understand."

"Me either," I said.

Jake joined in. "That makes three of us."

"Elliot," my dad started, "I'm a financial consultant. And Paramount Point, the company that owns the golf course, hired my company to come in and help turn the business around. So my boss sent me here as a consultant and controller to help Mr. Melton's golf course make a profit."

Suddenly, a wave of panic set in. The dots finally started connecting, and I realized that Marley's dad WAS the important client my dad was talking about. And if the golf course didn't become successful, he could be out of a job, too.

"So what happens if you can't get business going again?" I knew I was torturing myself, but I had to ask.

"Well," Mr. Melton looked at all of us with a sad face, "they want to tear down the golf course and sell it to developers to make more houses."

All I could think about was losing our cabin, or never coming to Vermont again, or worse, never seeing Marley again. My mind was bouncing all over the place. Jake gave me that best-friend kind of soft punch in the arm, as if to say, *Sorry, buddy.*

A sinking feeling filled me and I fought back the rush of water that tried to dive off my lower eyelids. *Do not blink, Elliot*, I told myself. *Do not blink.*

Me, Jake, and Marley glanced at each other. Her eyes looked a little red, too. We knew without speaking that we had no choice but to act.

And now, more than ever, I knew I HAD to come up with something. I HAD to save this golf course... for Marley...for Dad...for all of us.

CHAPTER FOURTEEN
The Cassie Catastrophe

The next morning, the sounds of voices woke Jake and me up. Sammy was playing with Tommy and ordering him around. And Mrs. Weber and Mom were blabbing about some new book they were reading. Then I heard Mom say she was coming to wake us up. Tommy's footsteps pounded after her.

She poked her head into our room. "Boys, why don't you get up? It's almost 10:00." Tommy pushed on Mom's rear, trying to shove past her. He was babbling some baby nonsense as usual.

"Minnoooows. Cheese at me," he said.

Jake sat up and giggled. "What's he saying?"

Mom combed her fingers through Tommy's hair. "He wants someone to take a picture of him," she said in that high-pitched voice that grownups use when they talk to babies.

"Take a picture? I don't get it," I said.

Tommy finally squeezed through the space between Mom and the doorway and wobbled over to Jake. He flopped himself on top of Jake with a thud.

"Oomph!" Jake exhaled, as he rolled backwards on the bed and took Tommy with him. Tommy giggled hard.

Mom continued to explain, talking a little louder now so you could hear over their *antics*. Mom uses that word antics a lot. It's a real word. "You see," she said, "earlier this morning, Sammy and Tyler were taking pictures of the minnows they set free. Tommy heard them telling the fish to 'say cheese,' and that's what started his latest obsession."

"Session! Session!" Tommy chanted.

"WHAT?!" I interrupted Jake's laugh and lurched forward from the top bunk. "She didn't use my camera, did—?"

"She did." Mom instantly silenced me.

"Are you kidding me? Who said she could—?"

"I said!" She gave me one of those looks that meant, *Ya got that buster?*

I got it alright. And I swallowed my next comment like a leftover brussels sprout.

"C'mon, Tommy. Let's go in and have some breakfast," she said, reaching her hand out to help him off of the bed. They left for the kitchen. "Don't forget to wash up," she called out to us. "It'll be ready in a minute."

"I can't believe it!" I said to Jake when they left. "Sammy used the camera. You know how she loses everything. And even more importantly, we have those pictures of the sea monster thing, and I wanted to download them onto the computer to get a close-up look. What if she erased them?"

"Don't worry, man," Jake said, as if he read my mind. "Sammy's almost in second grade. I bet she can probably press a button on a camera without causing too much trouble by now."

"I don't know about that." He didn't have me convinced.

We rushed through Mrs. Weber's super deluxe breakfast. In fact, I ate so fast and so much that I almost needed a forklift to get me out of the kitchen chair. I wanted to hurry up and find my camera, but the taste of those caramel pecan pancakes with real Vermont maple syrup and those bacon biscuit cheese twists were too good to pass up.

There was no time to waste. I had to locate the camera, and we had to come up with a much better plan if we were going to save the golf course and my dad's job.

Jake and I were supposed to meet Marley at noon to discuss a plan. If only we had a way to talk to Cassie before then. Cassie was chock-full of ideas. We've never been able to solve a problem without her help—she's like some kind of super genius or something. There was no phone in the cabin, and according to my parents, I'm not old enough to have a cell phone yet, even though half the kids in school have one by now, but I'll save that for another time.

I was about to ask if I could borrow Mom's cell phone when I noticed Dad's laptop sitting on the coffee table. "Duh!" I hit myself in the head. *Why didn't I think of that sooner?*

"Hey, Mom, does Dad need this laptop today?"

"No. He already left to meet with Mr. Melton."

"Is it okay if Jake and I go on the computer to instant message Cassie?"

"Yes. But not too long, honey. Whenever you use that program, the laptop gets locked up, and I don't want any of Dad's work to get deleted."

Jake logged on with his screen name, *Jakester011*.

We were in luck. In the friend's column, *ClassyCassy5 is online* was highlighted.

I typed her a message:

Jakester011: Heyy Cass. You There?

ClassyCassie5: Hiiii you guys!!! How's Vermont?

103

I started to type an answer, but Jake jumped in. "Let me do this or we'll be here all day." He shoved me over on the chair— I was hanging on by a butt cheek.

Jakester011: Good. But we have a problem. Need your help.

ClassieCassie5: Really??? Whats goin on?

Just then Sammy had to get her big nose in our business. Her flip-flops click-clacked across the den until she was right in my face. "What are you doing on Daddy's computer? Did he say you could use it?"

"We're talking to Cassie. Mom said we could. And where's my camera?"

"I don't know. It's in the house somewhere," she said. "But first I want to say hi to Cassie. Can I?"

"No way. Go and find my camera. We're working on something important, and I'm going to need it. And shouldn't you be out saving minnows or something, anyway?

"You're such a Jerky McJerk Pants!"

I slammed my head in my hands. I could tell Jake was laughing because his head was bobbing up and down like a chicken.

"So the instant message?" Jake said. "What should I say?"

"Just tell Cassie we have to save my dad's job and ask how we can get more business at the golf course. We

104

need ideas."

Jake typed like a madman. *How does he do that?*

Jakester011: The first day I got here we saw a weird creature in the lake. Then Elliot almost caught it when we were fishing. The thing was HUGE. Think it's a sea monster. We tried to get some pictures of it. Thing is freaky.

When I read the dialogue box, I said, "What are you doing? We need her to help us with the *golf course* problem. Not the sea monster." Then Cassie wrote back.

ClassieCassie5: No way! I just watched a show about that a few days ago. It was on the Loch Ness Monster.

It just figures she would have seen that documentary. Brainiac. Now I had two things to talk to her about. I hovered over Jake's shoulders. "C'mon. Ask about the golf course. And then ask for more info on the Loch Ness Monster."

"Okay. Okay."

Jake's fingers flew across the keyboard. And just before he hit *send*, I noticed he mentioned Marley.

Jakester011: Marley's dad is going to lose the golf course if more people don't start coming here. Elliot's dad is working with him. And he could lose his job, too. We have to help get more people to come here before the end of summer. Any ideas?

I slammed my hand on top of his. "No! Why are you telling her about Marley? Did it send?" The last thing I wanted was for Cassie to feel bad that we were investigating something with another girl. She might have thought we replaced her.

"Ohhhhhh. I get it," Jake said with a sneer. "You don't want Cassie to know about Marley."

"No. That's not it."

Then Cassie wrote back:

ClassieCassie5: Who's Marley???????????

"You see! I knew it," I said to Jake.

Jakester011: She's the girl next door.

She didn't answer. *Great.* I felt really bad. And I know Cassie. She would be upset and wouldn't talk to us for a while. Too much stuff was going on in my head. It felt like a balloon getting bigger and bigger until it was about to burst.

It was the longest five minutes I'd ever waited. Cassie still hadn't answered. I knew she was bugged by that comment. "How are we going to get out of this?" I asked Jake. "We need her help."

Just then, the computer sounded. Cassie finally responded. It was abrupt, but brilliant.

ClassieCassie5: Duh, you guys. Use your sea monster pictures. Get people curious. Look what happened at Loch Ness in Scotland. People still come from all over hoping to see it. GTG. BYE.

"Holy cow!" I looked at Jake. "THAT'S IT!"

CHAPTER FIFTEEN
Operation Save the Golf Course

I was worried that Cassie was mad at me, but at the same time, I was psyched about her idea, which led me to think of all the possibilities. Lake Bomoseen could be the next Loch Ness. Imagine people flocking here from all over to see the sea monster phenomenon. I couldn't wait to tell Marley. Imagine: a sea monster that saved a golf course.

Jake and I rushed next door and pounded until Marley answered.

"Elliot, Jake, you guys are early."

I didn't even wait for her to invite us in. I just pushed past her and pulled out a kitchen chair. "Here, you better sit down. We have it! We have the idea that's going to save the golf course." I pulled out another chair, turned it around, and sat down. Jake did the same.

"What? What is it?" She combed her hair with her fingers. I got distracted for a minute because I noticed she was still wearing the orange bracelet from yesterday. She must've forgotten she was wearing it. But that was cool because I wanted her to have it, but I didn't actually want her to know I was giving it to her, so it worked out perfectly.

"The sea monster!" I said.

"Yeah. What about it? How can that help my father's golf course?"

Jake chimed in, "Cassie gave us a great idea."

"Who's Cassie?" Marley looked confused.

"She's our friend from home and after talking to her, I came up with an awesome plan. We could give our sea monster a name…like how they have *Nessie* for Loch Ness, and *Champ* at Lake Champlain. We can come up with a name for Lake Bomoseen's sea monster. Then we could start circulating the pictures we have. People will freak!" Jake said.

"You might have something there." Marley shifted in her seat. "They'll get excited and curious. But did we print out our pictures? I think we need to see if we have a close-up shot."

"Oh crud!" I blurted, remembering the camera again. "Sammy still has the camera somewhere. We have to find it!"

"Don't worry. It'll be fine," she said. "It's got to be

around your house somewhere."

Just hearing her voice say that made me feel a little better. For now. Then I went back to the plan. The thought of it got me so pumped. "Do you realize how awesome this could be?" I said. "We can forget the whole fund raiser at the summer dance idea. Because once the buzz gets around that Lake Bomoseen has a sea monster, people will be flocking to the lake."

"Or running for the hills," added Jake. "Who wants to swim in a lake with a monster in it? Not me!"

Marley shrugged. "So, that still doesn't help the golf course."

I shook my head. "C'mon, you guys, sea monsters aren't predators or anything. They just live in the lake, you know, and eat fish. It's more of an exciting thing than a scary thing."

Marley nodded. "Okay, you do have a point."

Jake jumped in again. "Wait! That's where the souvenir idea comes in handy."

"Souvenirs?" Marley asked.

"YES!" I slammed the back of my chair with excitement.

Jake continued, "We could have T-shirts and Frisbees and stuff with illustrations of the sea monster on them. And we can make the sea monster look really friendly, and even cute. Your dad can set up a gift area in the pro shop. It's just like we read on one of the Loch Ness websites. They opened a whole souvenir shop of *Nessie* stuff."

"Wouldn't it be cool if there was a mini golf course with a see monster theme, too?" I shouted over the two of them.

Marley gasped. Her eyes grew twice their size. Jake looked at me.

"What?" I shrugged in embarrassment. "I was just kidding."

"Kidding? Are you crazy?" Marley blurted. "That's perfect!" She threw her arms around me and practically knocked me off the chair. I'm certain my heart stopped beating for a second. I was in heaven.

She jumped up after hugging me. "This is fantabulous!" she said, turning to Jake.

Here we go with those made-up words again. "Between you two and Sammy, you could start writing your own dictionary," I teased. "Seriously, you have like a whole new language already."

Marley laughed. Then she threw her arms around Jake, too. I hate to admit it, but watching Marley hug Jake made a microscopic amount of jealousy leak out. At least his hug wasn't as long as my hug.

"You guys are the best!" Marley said. "Those are awesome ideas. We have to get as many pictures as possible. And the mini golf course idea...we have to tell my dad. There are no good mini golf courses around here. But let's think. How can we get these pictures to people?"

"On our bikes?" Jake suggested.

Marley jumped out of her chair. "I KNOW! What if we send a picture with a little write-up to *The Lakeside Herald?* That's the local town newspaper. I can write it. If that story gets in the paper, everyone will go crazy."

"Holy crud!" We all high-fived.

She twisted her mouth to one side. "One little problem, though," she said. "The paper only comes out once a month. So, we'll have to get our story in the July issue if it's going to do us any good."

"But it's already June 26th. That gives us only four days to get better pictures and write the article," I said.

Marley winced. "Not exactly."

Jake piped in, "Why not?"

She tucked her fingertips in her shorts pockets. "You can't just send an article to a newspaper the day before it comes out. They have to edit it and plan the layout. Like, where it's going to go, and stuff like that."

"How do you know that?" Jake asked.

"Because before my parents got divorced, my mother worked for *The Lakeside Herald.* She's a journalist."

I threw my hands up in the air. "That gives us even

less time!"

Jake's eyes bugged out.

"Don't get discouraged so easily," Marley said. "I know from going to work with my mother that if they get a really good story a few days before the paper goes to print, there's a chance it could still get in."

"I guess it can't hurt to try," I said. But then panic set in. "But we're gonna have to hustle."

"Exactly!" Marley said. "We need to get the Million-Dollar Photo of our sea monster. So let's keep the camera with us at all times. And when we get the perfect sighting, we snap 'til we drop."

"Wait. The camera. Are Tyler and Sammy still setting the minnows free?" I asked.

"Yup. They were at it this morning," Marley said. "And look. There's the table out front. I think they're setting up to sell more stuff today."

"Remember what you said yesterday about dusting off the big poles?" I said. "You're right. If they've been dumping buckets of minnows for two days, then I bet there will be a lot more bass lurking around the dock—"

"And more bass might mean a better chance of getting the sea monster in the area." Marley finished my sentence.

"Then our next mission is to meet at the dock," I said.

"In the meantime, maybe we can help Sammy and Tyler get more minnows and set them free," Jake suggested. "More minnows means more bait."

I looked at Marley. "What do you think?"

She nodded. "It's a plan."

"I'll help them man the table," Jake offered.

I poked Jake's shoulder. "Are you chickening out?"

"No." Jake got all twitchy. "I'm not a chicken. I just think Sammy and Tyler would be more willing to let *me* help them than you guys. Besides, they'd know you were up to something."

He had a point. "Good thinking, Jakester."

"No problemo," he said. And that was a real word, even if it was Spanish.

"Okay. I'll go get the camera and start downloading the pictures onto the laptop. Jake, you go schmooze Sammy and Tyler and get them to let you help."

Marley stood up to walk us to the door. "And I'll start working on the letter to the newspaper."

This whole thing was strange. And as much as I wanted to save the golf course, I had a twisted feeling in my stomach that we were headed for a very extraordinary evening.

CHAPTER SIXTEEN
Kerplunk

"Where is that camera?" I pushed around a stack of books and the bag of Gummy Worms. "Sammy said it was in the house somewhere." It wasn't on the desk where I always kept it. Then I checked the kitchen. "Mom, is my camera in here?" She was giving Tommy chicken nuggets.

"I don't see it, Elliot. Where did you leave it?"

"ME? Didn't you say Sammy was using it this morning?" I huffed on my way back into the den and flipped over the couch cushions. "What did she do with it?!" I looked in every nook and cranny.

I marched back into the kitchen again. "I have to find it, Mom."

"Maybe she put it in her room," she answered without looking up from Tommy.

"Cheese at me. Cheese at me?" Tommy blabbed, spitting pieces of chicken everywhere.

I couldn't even laugh because I was getting steamed. Every single time Sammy touched my stuff, it got lost or ruined or whatever. And this was not the time to have my camera go missing.

I looked over every inch of the one-by-two kitchen. While I was hunting, Mom pointed at me, and in a high-pitched voice asked Tommy, "Who's that?" Tommy tried to say "Elliot," only it came out as "Idiot." That made me stop and chuckle.

Next, I went into Sammy's bedroom and looked on her bed. The only thing there was a bunch of string and a box of beads. I put them on the floor and yanked the covers off. Then I checked underneath. I searched the floor, the closet, and in her suitcase. "Where could it be?!" My blood was pulsing in my neck. I didn't have time for this. Those pictures were our only hope right now. I needed that camera.

I ran into my room and checked both bunks. Nothing. By this point I was frantic. I ran back out to the kitchen.

"Maybe she left it on the porch," Mom said, sensing my panic. "Or on the grass. Or for that matter, why don't you just go find her and ask her?"

I didn't even answer. I just rushed through the den and whipped open the screen door, letting it slam hard behind me. The only things on the porch were some bathing suits and beach towels hanging over the balcony, and the fishing poles in the corner. "THIS STINKS!"

I hopped down the stairs and bolted around front to find Jake. I didn't see anyone at the sale table. "Jake, are you out here?" I shouted.

Roxy came charging over, barking like crazy. I braced myself for the slobber attack, but she zipped right past me and ran toward the water. *That's strange,* I thought.

Jake popped his head up from behind the table. "Oh, hey."

"What are you doing down there?"

He shook his head. "I knocked the jar of money over, so now I'm picking about a million dimes and nickels and quarters out of the grass."

"Ha, ha. Nice going," I laughed. "Seriously, man. I can't find the stupid camera. I searched the whole darn cabin. Do you know where Sammy is?"

"She's down at the dock with Tyler and my mom. They're dumping the minnows again."

"I gotta go find out what she did with it."

"Can you believe they're making so much money on this stuff?" Jake picked up a bracelet. "I have to learn how to make these things."

"Did you seriously just say you want to make bracelets?" I shook my head.

"What?" He held his hands out. "It's a good money maker."

I smiled. "Be right back."

I hustled down to the dock. Mrs. Weber was sitting on the grass, watching Tyler and Sammy. "The kids are saving minnows," she laughed.

Sam and Tyler were busy waving goodbye. Then I saw Sammy holding MY camera.

"What are you doing with my camera again?" I bellowed across the yard. "I've been looking all over for it."

"I'm taking pictures of the fishies."

Roxy was still barking like mad at something off the big dock where my dad's boat was tied up.

"I need it back. Give it to me." By now I was huffing and stomping. Roxy's barking got louder. She never barks for that long. Usually it's a quick hello and that's it. I got curious and walked over to explore what was going on. Roxy was crouched down and looking out onto the lake. "What is it, Roxy? Whatcha seeing out there, girl?" *Uh oh,* I thought. My insides did that swirly thing.

"Sam," I said extra slow and drawn out. "Hurry up with that camera, will ya?"

"I'm not done yet," she squealed.

Roxy's barking was creeping me out. The little hairs

on my arms stuck up. "Hurry!"

I kept my eyes fixed on the water, looking for any weird ripples on the surface. There was some bubbling a few hundred feet out from the dock, like something was about to surface. I felt beads of sweat forming on my forehead. Then I saw a big gray shadow moving on the top of the lake.

"QUICK!" I shrieked. "SAM! I need the camera. NOW!"

"What is it?" Mrs. Weber called out.

"I don't know." A lump rose in my throat and I pointed to the water. "There's something out there. Find Dad! Get Jake!" My voice cracked.

The first hump surfaced on the water. "SAMMY, THE CAMERA!"

Jake came flying down the hill, followed by Marley.

A black neck emerged from the lake, rising higher and higher. This time it didn't have the beige beak thing. It looked like the platypus head we saw on the boat the other day. The neck kept going. I swear its neck was as tall as my dad. I was frozen in place and my mouth was bone dry, like all the moisture was sucked out of my tongue. All I could think was, *This is the million dollar shot!*

"SAMMY, NOW!" I wailed. "GIMME THE CAMERA!" I had my hand out like I was waiting for a baton in a relay race.

Sammy saw the creature and went ballistic. "Eek! It's the sea monster!"

Tyler took a flying leap off the dock and ran home. Mrs. Weber stood up. "Now kids, don't panic," she shouted as she paced on the grass. She squinted her eyes. "What's going on out there?"

Marley and Jake were screaming to Sammy, "Give us the camera!" Sammy slipped off the dock and fell on the grass.

"GET UP! GET UP!" I was screaming my head off now. The sea monster was still above water.

Marley tried to grab Sammy's hand, but Sammy ran toward me. Jake chased her and got too close to the water's edge. He slipped on a slimy rock and fell into the edge of the lake.

"Ow! My finger!" Jake shouted. Then he must've realized he was in the water with that thing because he screamed like a lunatic, "Ahhhh! Get me out of here!" he yelled frantically, flailing and splashing in about two inches of water.

"You okay?" I called, my eyes darting between him and the sea monster.

Mrs. Weber ran to his side.

I heard Sammy clomping onto my dock. I turned to face her, and without giving me a chance to get ready, she hurled the camera at me. "HERE!" she shouted.

I leapt in the air to catch it, but it was too far from my reach, and the camera plummeted into the lake. By that point Sammy was crying and running back to the house.

I stood in shock as I watched our only hope sink to the bottom of Lake Bomoseen.

CHAPTER SEVENTEEN
The Camera Fiasco

I watched the camera sink and then looked back to where the sea monster was. But it was gone. I really wanted to jump in and get the camera, but I was sort of afraid, even though I kept telling everyone that sea monsters are harmless. The sea monster hadn't been that far away from the dock a few minutes earlier. My hands shook.

I didn't realize that Jake was really hurt. Everyone ran down and surrounded him: Mr. Melton and my dad, along with my mom and Mrs. Weber. I wanted to run down there too, but I was hypnotized, looking into the water, and wondering how to get my camera back.

Just then Marley touched me on the shoulder. I gasped. "What are we going to do now?" her voice trailed off.

I took off my socks and shoes. Then my shirt. And even though I was focused on the sea monster and the camera, I still felt the urge to suck in my stomach so my abs looked good in front of Marley.

"We missed our chance at the million dollar shot," I said. "So whatever is on this camera, if it's still there, is all we have." I was about to jump in.

"Wait." Marley said. "You're going in there? With that creature?!"

"I have to," I said. "It's our last hope."

"Okay," she said. "If you say so." She hopped onto Dad's boat, wobbled over to the back, and snatched a pair of goggles hanging off the side. Then she chucked them to me. "Here. You might need these."

I stretched the goggles over my head, and took the plunge, hoping that I wouldn't end up as the sea monster's afternoon snack. I swam and kicked until I saw the bottom. Lucky thing the lake is shallow right next to the dock. I can actually stand up if I go on my tippy tippy toes. I struggled to hold my breath and pawed around at the bottom. I scratched and grabbed handfuls of weeds and dirt. Then I saw the camera and felt for the strap. I tried to loop it around my wrist, but I needed to get some air. I pushed my feet off the bottom as hard as I could until I shot straight out of the water and gasped.

"Are you okay?" Marley shouted. "Did you get it?"

"Not yet." I sucked in some air and went back down. I felt around the bottom, grasping handfuls of green, grassy muck until I found the strap again. This time it was stuck on something. I tugged and pulled until a weed pulled out of the bottom, and the camera yanked free. Then I catapulted myself off the bottom and broke the surface.

"Here!" I blew out a huge breath. "Grab this."

Marley took the camera from me, and I hurdled myself up over the side of the dock. She shook the water from the camera, pulled out the memory card, and gave it to me. I blew on it and shoved it in my sopping wet pocket. Like that helped. Then we ran over to Jake.

"Are you okay, buddy?"

My parents were pointing into the water.

Mrs. Weber was kneeling with Jake. Marley's dad knelt down next to them and asked Jake to try to make a fist. He couldn't even bend his fingers. Oh, man! They looked all bluish green and swollen already. "Nice color," I said, trying to make him laugh. "It goes with your shirt."

Jake looked up at me. "Hugebungous fingers, huh?"

I had to laugh. "Add that to your dictionary," I said.

"That was sick, wasn't it?" Jake said to Marley.

I nodded, still in disbelief.

Marley's dad whispered something to Mrs. Weber. Then he spoke up. "I think he needs to have this x-rayed. I'll drive Peg and Jake over to the hospital."

Mrs. Weber nodded. "I'll go get my purse."

Jake and I looked at each other. *Marley's Dad's taking them? What was up with that?*

"See ya later, Jake. I hope it's not broken," I told him as Mr. Melton helped him up. "That would totally stink."

"Yeah," Marley added.

Jake raised his arm and waved goodbye with his good hand. "I hope it's not broken, too."

Marley and I raced up to the house. By the time we got there, we were both out of breath.

"That neck was like five feet long!" she yelled.

"I can't believe I blew it. Getting the pictures, I mean. We'll never get that close to it again."

"We might." She faked a hopeful smile.

We decided to go over what was left of our plan—now that the camera had taken a plunge—while we were waiting for Jake to get back. I mean, I didn't think we could salvage the memory card after it did the backstroke. And our deadline for the newspaper was approaching faster than a snowball rolling down hill.

"Lets check out the memory card," I said. "I'll see if

my Dad can help when he gets back from the hospital. Do you want to get something to eat?"

Marley and I went inside the house and passed Dad in the den. "Dad, you're here!" I blurted. "I thought you went to the hospital, too."

"No. Mrs. Weber and Mr. Melton took Jake," Dad said. "That's plenty." He was sunk in his favorite recliner doing a crossword puzzle. "That was quite a scene, huh?"

"Yeah. Did you see that?!" I said.

"Not really," Dad shook his head. "Bill and I walked in at the tail end, no pun intended." He laughed.

"I don't care what anyone says, Dad, there is definitely a sea monster out there!"

"Why don't we gather all the facts first before making any assumptions? It could be a big fish or some rare form of aquatic life."

"Assumptions?" Dad was always so calm, it made me nuts.

I stomped to the kitchen with Marley and threw together some peanut butter sandwiches, grabbed two sodas, and we hustled back to the porch.

While Marley and I ate, we tried to think of something. "Do you think any of the pictures are still good? I mean... does the memory card get ruined when it's wet?" It was a good question, because I hadn't ever dropped my camera in the water before, so I didn't know for sure. She just shrugged.

I knelt on my chair and peeked through the porch screen to see how involved Dad was. Usually, once he's in a crossword, you can't get him out for hours. "Hey, Dad." I waited for him to look up. He did. *Jackpot.* "You think it's possible to get any of the pictures off a memory card that was dropped in the lake, or is it ruined?"

"Do you have it?" he asked, raising his glasses.

I showed him through the screen. "Right here."

He folded the paper closed. "Let me have a look."

"Yes!" I untwisted myself and jumped off the chair. "C'mon Marley."

I sat down at the desk, and he told me where to plug the memory card into the laptop. Then, he showed me how to download the files. A little box popped open on the screen. It read, *Unable to Access Files.* "Must be water damage," Dad said.

Marley's shoulders slumped. I didn't want her to think I screwed up. "Sorry," I said, pulling a thread that was hanging off my shorts.

She pushed my hand. "You're going to unravel yourself," she joked. "It's not your fault." But I felt like it was. I felt like I was a failure with a capital *F*.

"Wait." Dad leaned over my shoulder and typed on the keyboard. "Here are some of the pictures from our fishing trip." Marley lunged between us to get a peek. Now, how was I supposed to concentrate when she smelled like delicious cotton candy? I don't know how, but I managed to focus on the muddled pictures, anyway. "This one might be salvageable," Dad said. I thought he was just being nice. It really wasn't that great. It was more like a big shadow.

"What about the ones we got near Myron's?" I tried to stay hopeful, but it wasn't looking good. We did find one, but it was so far away, it was hard to see. "Maybe we can blow this one up."

Marley agreed. "That's a great idea."

We looked through some more, but most of them were blurry.

"Do we have a printer here?" I asked Dad.

"Yes. I put the portable one in the bedroom for work."

I kept on clicking pictures. None of them were any good.

"Hold on," Dad said, scanning each one like he was looking for a missing puzzle piece. Every time I tried to open a file, we would get another annoying message like *Unable to Open File* or *File Not Available*. And one time it said, *A System Error has Occurred*. And then the whole dumb laptop shut down.

It was looking pretty bleak in the picture department. I couldn't believe all the pictures were ruined. Well, all but two, but they were fuzzy at best. It seemed there would be no chances of proving there was a sea monster, or of helping the golf course.

"Dad, why don't we just forget—"

Sammy burst into the house like a wild bronco, interrupting my sentence. "Watcha looking at? Can I see?" she asked. I know she was trying to be nice since I was so mad about the camera.

Tommy toddled in behind her. "Idiot!" he shouted and made a beeline right for me. He slammed into my back and gave me a hug. I laughed because his stumpy little arms barely made it around my sides.

"Aw, he's so cute," Marley said. She picked him up and balanced him on her hip.

"Can I look, too?" Sammy asked.

"Shh," I said, but not as snottily as I wanted to. "We're trying to get the pictures off the camera." What I really wanted to say was, *the camera YOU dropped in the lake and ruined for us,* but I didn't want her to feel any worse than she already did. I mean... I know she's a pain and all, but I kind of felt bad that she was really scared of the monster. And, well, she's my little sister, you know. But I wasn't about to tell her all that.

Sammy tugged on Dad's arm. "Did you see any of my pictures? Where are my minnow pictures?"

"Just a minute, Sam," he said.

I really wasn't in the mood to be looking at pictures of minnows, but I nodded to Dad to click on a few just to get it over with.

The front door banged and then I heard voices. I called out, "Hey, is that Jake?"

Marley looked up. "I think so. It sounds like my father's voice."

A few seconds later, Jake peeked his head into the den. The rest of him was hiding behind the kitchen wall. "Check this out." He slowly moved his hand into view. "I broke two fingers."

I jumped up. "GET OUT!" I said. "They're actually broken? Come here. Let me see."

Mom, Mrs. Weber and Mr. Melton stayed in the kitchen. I got so distracted checking out Jake's fingers that I didn't notice Dad had scooted in my seat and had pulled up another picture on the monitor. Marley flicked me on the arm to get my attention.

"Huh? What?"

"Holy cow!" Jake said, pointing his taped-up hand toward the computer. On the screen was a cockeyed, sort of sideways picture with the sea monster in the background. If you looked at it with your head almost upside down, it was an unbelievable, amazing, picture of the sea monster with its neck jutting out of the water. And, even though it was a little far away, it was pretty clear. I couldn't believe my eyes.

"Let's turn this around," Dad said. A few more clicks, and he managed to turn it right side up. "Hmph." He was glued to it. He took his glasses off and then put them on again.

I practically sat on his lap to get a closer look. "Where did that come from? I...I didn't take that picture," I said. "It looks like the ones from those websites we were looking at."

Jake's jaw opened so wide, I could see his tonsils. Marley perked up too. "That's the Million-Dollar Picture!"

Sammy poked at the screen. "Hey, that's MY picture."

"*Your* picture?" I said. "What do you mean, *your* picture?"

Sammy took a big gulp of breath as she explained, "See the minnows in the front? That's my picture, but it's all messed up now. See," she continued, "I was trying to take pictures of my minnows but then you were yelling at me because I had the camera so I was just hurrying up and then the monster scared me because Mommy said there wasn't supposed to be a monster in the lake and...Tyler was telling me to press the button and the camera was moving and I didn't want the monster in my minnow pictures," she paused, a long pause, and then got real quiet... "And I guess the monster got in there by an accident."

I was so excited, I couldn't contain myself. I scooped

up Sammy and hugged her with all my might. "Sammy, that is the best accident you've ever had!"

Jake displayed his busted-up fingers. "Even better than my accident," he said.

"You rock, Sammy!" I said, swinging her around. And at that moment, I totally meant it. Marley and Jake joined in, and we were all hugging and dancing in the den. For a second I wondered how weird we actually looked.

Marley messed up Sam's hair. "You just saved our plan."

"I did?" Sam looked so proud of herself. "What did I do? What plan?"

I noticed Dad was still examining the picture. He had his face so close to the monitor, I thought he was going to kiss it.

"Me too," Dad said, not taking his eyes off the monitor. "I'd like to know what that plan is, too."

CHAPTER EIGHTEEN

Bo

We never told Dad our plan, because we hadn't really put anything into motion yet. Not for real, anyway. I couldn't wait to send the pictures to the paper. I printed out Sammy's accident picture, along with the two barely visible ones that I was able to salvage from the waterlogged camera.

The next morning Jake and I skipped breakfast so we could get to Marley's. And believe me, passing up Mrs. Weber's cooking was not an easy thing to do. Especially when she made strawberry banana crepes with whipped cream on top. Yum.

We wanted to hurry and get to Marley's so we could finish up the package for *The Lakeside Herald*. I clutched the three photographs between my fingers like a vice grip. No way was I letting these get away. Especially the

Million-Dollar Shot.

As soon as I opened the door and stepped outside, the humid summer air punched me in the chest. A mist rose above the lake, and the sun was low in the sky. It was quiet. Then I heard faint guitar sounds.

"Jake, that's Marley. Let's go."

We mumbled a quick hello as we passed her grandmother in the kitchen and bolted to Marley's room. When we got there, I couldn't help but notice that her room was decorated like one of those TV shows, with fluorescent orange and pink walls and fur beanbag chairs. Everything matched perfectly. Even her pen matched the room.

"Cool room," I said.

"Thanks."

"Hey, what's your fish's name?" Jake asked. Marley had a fish tank with lime green rocks and a pink background with purple and blue rocks on the bottom. A small goldfish swam around.

"Peeve," she said.

"Peeve?" I crinkled my forehead. "That's odd for a fish."

"Not really," she said. "It's my pet peeve."

Jake rolled onto his elbows and cracked up. "That's a good one." We all had a good laugh. But then it was time to focus.

Marley had already taken out her article and laid the pages over the floor. Jake and I sat cross-legged next to her. And I put the photographs next to us.

Jake moved around the pages. "You wrote the whole thing already? How'd you do that, Marley?" he asked.

"I couldn't sleep after everything that happened last night," Marley said, "so I stayed up and wrote this. Then I got up this morning and typed it all out. I had to get it done while Tyler was still asleep or he would have hogged the computer."

Jake and I read the article. It was amazing. She wrote about how we were visiting Lake Bomoseen and came upon a visitor, an unexpected visitor. "This is great!" Jake blurted.

"Thanks. Only thing is we have to come up with a name for the sea monster, remember?"

"Oh yeah," I said. "That's right."

We tossed around a bunch of lame ideas, like, Mosey, and The Bomb. Then Jake blurted, "How about Bo?"

"I love it! Bo!" Marley squealed. "It's perfect. Don't you think so, Elliot?"

"Totally!"

She gathered up all the papers and smoothed out her shirt. "I'm going to make these changes and print it out. Then we can get it in the mail to *The Lakeside Herald* office. They'll have it by tomorrow."

When Marley came back, we attached the article to the pictures. Then Marley put a handwritten note on the front:

My name is Marley Melton, and my mother Ava used to be a journalist for your paper. I know the deadline for July has probably passed, but here is an article and some pictures that my friends and I thought you'd be interested in.

Sincerely,

Marley A. Melton, Elliot Stone, and Jake Weber

Marley sealed the envelope and the three of us sped out of the house, hopped on our bikes, and took off like lightning. We headed straight for the nearest mailbox.

Now all we had to do was wait and see what would happen. *Would they print our article and pictures? What if they didn't? Then what would we do?*

CHAPTER NINETEEN
No News is Good News. Or is it?

It was July 1st. A big day. Not only was it the day of Cassie's party, but it was also the day *The Lakeside Herald*'s July issue would be coming out. I waited by the front window for Dad to come back from his morning coffee run. Mom makes coffee at the cabin, but Dad likes to go out and get his coffee from Myron's because they have flavored coffees like blueberry and hazelnut.

I saw him pull up and get out of the car, and he didn't have a newspaper with him. That was weird.

"Did you get the paper?" I asked nonchalantly when he came in. I was dying to see if they'd put our story in there.

"No. Myron said they didn't get the delivery yet. I'll check back later. Why? You looking for something in particular?"

"Nah. Just wondering." *I guess we didn't make it. There won't be an article, no pictures, the golf course will close down, Mr. Melton and Dad will be out of jobs, and I'll be outta here before you could say sea monster.*

Dad put together a bunch of work papers and headed out. "I'm going to meet Bill at the golf course. You want to come up there later? We can pick you kids up around lunchtime. We'll play a few rounds of golf, and then you can hang out at the snack bar."

At first I was going to say flat out NO to golfing, but then I thought about it. *This might be the perfect opportunity for us to unveil our plans to Dad and Mr. Melton. If they were on board with us, it might actually work.*

Since Marley wasn't at my house yet and Jake was still sleeping, I had to make an executive decision in the best interest of our plan.

"Sure Dad," I said. "That'll be cool. I'll tell Jake when he gets up."

"Great. Be ready around noon," he said.

"Before you go, can I use your laptop to instant message Cassie? Today's her party." I had to contact her. I hadn't written back to her since the day she got mad at us. And, after all, it was her idea that got us going.

"Yes, but make sure you log out before you turn it off."

"Okay. Thanks, Dad."

As soon as he left, I signed on to see if Cassie's screen

name came up. It did. So I sent her a message:

Elliot1020: Are you there?

ClassyCassie5: Hey!

Elliot1020: Today's the big day.

ClassyCassie5: Yeah. Busy getting ready.

Elliot1020: Are you still mad at me?

ClassyCassie5: Wasn't really mad. Just wondering who Marley was and why it was a big secret.

Elliot1020: It wasn't a big secret. Just didn't want you to get mad that we were working on a mission without you. You're still our right hand man (girl). We had no choice. My dad's job was in jeopardy. Is in jeopardy.

ClassyCassie5: Oh. Ok.

Elliot1020: Besides, your idea rocked. And we used it to come up with a plan. We sent the pictures to the newspaper. Waiting to see if they print our story. And I'm still bummed about missing your party. Sorry.

ClassyCassie5: REALLY??? You think the idea was good? I hope it works. I'm sorry too. We miss you here. Mom says hi. And, "right hand man" works fine.

Elliot1020: Totally! I'll keep you posted as soon as I know something. Don't have too much fun without me. Check in later. Hi back.

Phew! I was so glad I got that settled. I thought I had hurt her feelings. And that felt pretty terrible. I mean it's not as if I like her or anything like that. We're just friends.

I hung around until Jake got up. While I waited, I made a list of things to tell our dads later. Like the pictures and letter to the newspaper, and naming the sea monster, and even the souvenir shop idea. Mom and Mrs. Weber took the little kids down to the water. Jake finally made an appearance.

"It's aliiiive," I said to Jake.

He rubbed his eyes and reached for a box of Cocoa Crunchies. "Uhhh," he groaned.

We only had an hour until Dad was coming back for us. As soon as Jake got his bowl of cereal poured, Marley knocked on the door. She bounced in the house wearing a lime green shirt and white shorts. Funny how all her shirts were sherbet colors. And this was the second time I saw her wearing the orange bracelet. It felt pretty cool.

While Jake ate his cereal, we decided that going to the golf course was perfect. We would have a captive audience in the car and tell them our plans. Jake and Marley agreed that if both dads thought our ideas were good, then we'd have more of us working on saving the golf course and more chances of being successful. Besides, this was my chance to prove I wasn't a little kid anymore.

Just then, I heard a car horn beep. "They're here," I said.

Jake slurped down the rest of his milk, wiped his mouth with his arm, and put the bowl in the sink. Marley got up and held the door for him. "You only have one usable hand, so you can go first." We bolted out to the car where Dad was waiting.

"Where's my father?" Marley asked.

"He'll be right back," Dad said.

Then we saw Mr. Melton talking to Jake's mom. He kissed her on the cheek and came back to the car. I gave Jake a swift elbow to the ribs. "Did you see that?"

"Yeah!" He elbowed me back.

When we drove a good distance away from the cabin, I eyeballed Marley and Jake to see if it was a good time to bring it up. I got the nods.

"So Dad. I...um, we... actually, wanted to tell you something. Well, both of you. You and Mr. Melton."

Marley's father looked over the headrest. And Dad talked to us through the rearview mirror. "What's on your mind?"

"We kind of had an idea to help the golf course. You know with the sea monster and all." My palms were getting all sweaty, and my heart did that thing it does when I'm about to get in trouble.

"Ahhh," Dad said. "This is the *plan* you kids were talking about last night."

Jake cleared his throat. "Um, yeah. And it's really

good."

"Really, Dad," Marley added.

"So let's hear it," Mr. Melton said.

"You know how we saw that creature in the water, and then we almost caught it when we were fishing, and again when we were near Myron's and then you saw it yesterday?"

"Yeah. But you can't be sure it was a sea monster, Elliot," Dad said. "There are a lot of explanations for what it could have been. I've been trying to figure it out."

"I'm not finished yet, Dad." I felt myself getting defensive.

"Sorry. Go ahead."

"Well, you saw the pictures last night, right? So me and Jake and Marley thought it would be a great idea to send them to *The Lakeside Herald* with an article, and then if they put the story in the paper, people would be going crazy to see the sea monster and want to spend time here at the lake."

"What?!" Dad yelled.

"Wait!" Marley chimed in. "There's more. Once we get the people coming here for the sea monster, which we named *Bo* by the way—"

"And," Jake interrupted, "we can set up souvenirs in the pro shop and everything. You know, like the things we saw online. The T-shirts and baseball caps, and cups and stuff."

"Plus," I added, "I even had an awesome idea to build a sea monster themed mini-golf course right on the regular golf course or next to it. Then kids will want to come here, too."

We were on fire. How could they not love our ideas? I saw Dad look at Mr. Melton and raise his eyebrows.

"Well?" I said, hopeful. "Any comments?"

"Elliot," Dad said, "those ideas are all really creative and thoughtful…" I knew a "but" was coming. "But I don't think you kids should send anything to the newspaper just yet, because you don't know for sure if there's a creature in that water and you don't want to create a panic for no reason."

My stomach felt sick. I looked up at Jake and Marley. None of us dared to open our mouths and say we'd already sent it.

CHAPTER TWENTY
Uh Oh. Now What?

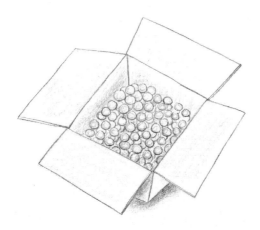

"But DAD!" I argued. "How can you say that wasn't a sea monster? You saw it. You saw the pictures."

"Pictures are deceiving. And, I spent a lot of time studying the few pictures that were salvaged. I think I may know what it was."

"What? You know what it was?" Jake asked.

"I think it may have been Soggy Joe," Dad said. "You remember that Soggy Joe's Balls and Tees stand?"

Okay, now Dad was flipping me out. "How could that have been Soggy Joe and why would he be in the lake looking like a sea monster? Explain that."

"Soggy Joe is a scuba diver," Dad said.

Marley, Jake, and I grimaced at the same time.

"He dives in the lake to collect all the golf balls that people have hit in the water. Then he sells them at his little shack on the side of the road."

I practically jumped out of my seatbelt. "What? All those used golf balls that he sells come from the bottom of the lake? But…but…I don't get it."

"Listen. I could see from some of the pictures that what you saw as a neck could be explained as Joe's pole and the beak was the net he uses to scoop up the golf balls. The black humps rolling on top of the water and the flippers were probably when he came up to the surface and went back down again. So you don't want to go causing a stir for no reason."

"But…that's impossible, Dad."

"It can't be." Jake shook his head. "I saw the thing with my own two eyes."

Marley nodded her head in agreement. "Me too. I saw it, too. You guys didn't see when it surfaced by the dock. That was no scuba diver!"

"I'll show you," Dad said. "Soggy Joe's is just up ahead."

I didn't want to believe that what we had seen was just a plain old scuba diver. *It couldn't be.* "We've been here a million times before and nobody ever mentioned Soggy Joe diving," I said.

"Elliot," Dad started. "Think about it. You've never been interested in golf, and Joe never had that shack before. He used to sell them from his house. I guess he's trying to get more business, too."

I refused to believe it. But then we pulled up to the little shack, Dad made us get out and meet Soggy Joe.

"Hey, Joe," Dad said as he paid for a box of golf balls. He held up the box and shook it. "Can you show the kids your gear, and tell them how you dive to get these?"

"Absolutely!" he said. Then he disappeared to the back of his little shack. He came out a few minutes later with scuba gear, and a big long pole thing with the net thing on the end. Just like the sea monster. My hopes shriveled like a rotten watermelon.

"I put on my wet suit," Joe explained, "and use this net so I can scoop down to the bottom and get as many golf balls as possible. You'd be surprised how many are down there. I usually dive right around the cliff, because that's where all the balls go over, but lately I've been diving around the island to see if I can find any other interesting artifacts as well."

"How can this possibly be?" I whispered to my friends. "Didn't it look like a real sea monster?"

Marley sighed. "I hate to say it, but the beak did look an awful lot like his net. If you think about it, you can see it in the picture."

"But Jake, you saw it with the binoculars, right?" I pressed on.

"Well, now I don't know. It could have been him, I guess."

"But what about yesterday?" I insisted. "Are you telling me yesterday it was Joe too?" I was sure I wasn't imagining things.

Jake just shrugged.

This was terrible. *Now what were we going to do?* We had already sent the pictures to the paper.

Dad thanked Soggy Joe and, as we were about to get in the car, he stopped. "Hey guys, I'm sorry to burst your bubble. I really do appreciate what you were trying to do."

Mr. Melton agreed. "I think it's really great that you kids all came together to try to help me. But we'll come up with something. Just not a sea monster."

My shoulders sank.

"Don't worry," Mr. Melton said. "We have some of our own ideas brewing too."

Dad changed the subject. "Hey, you kids want to grab some ice cream at Myron's before we hit the golf course?"

I had one hand on the car door handle and was staring down at the dirt. A shrug was about all I could muster up.

"Ice cream? Sure!" Jake said.

"Okay," Marley agreed.

Great. I wasn't really in the mood for ice cream. Not after all our ideas were kicked to the curb. I went along anyway. It felt like the golf course was slipping away, along with my dad's job and Marley's dad's, too.

The five of us waited for a couple of cars to go by and then dashed across the street to Myron's. The bells on the door jingled like crazy as we piled into the shop. The place was super busy, and there was a crowd around the counter.

The smell was so incredible that my appetite for ice cream came back. As I listened to the hum of chatting people, I thought I heard one of them say something about a monster and scooted myself a little closer so I could hear what they were saying. That's when I caught a glimpse of the fully stacked newspaper stand. I took one look and nearly fainted. Jake did a double take, and Marley's eyes grew as big as pancakes. I held up a copy of *The Lakeside Herald*. Dad and Mr. Melton looked at the same time.

On the cover was our sea monster picture, big as day. Above it in big letters:

LAKE BOMOSEEN HAS A VISITOR!!! Story on page 5.

CHAPTER TWENTY-ONE
The Sea Monster is Out of the Bag

I wasn't sure exactly what to do. It was too late to make up excuses for why we didn't tell them we'd already sent it.

"So," Dad said, all serious. "I see you kids went ahead with the plan before you told us about it."

I choked back the growing lump in my throat. Suddenly, ice cream didn't seem so appetizing again. Heat traveled up my neck and up to my ears. I bet if you looked closely enough you would have seen smoke coming out of them. I didn't even want to look up at Jake or Marley because my eyes were filling up, and crying in front of Marley was definitely not an option.

I pulled Dad over to the side. "I'm really sorry, Dad," I whispered. "I didn't think it was...I mean I thought we were helping."

"I know." He rubbed my head. "It's okay, Elliot. But

I wish you would have told me."

Marley must've had the same idea because she was whispering to her father, too.

"Look," Mr. Melton said. "You kids did a great thing for us, but because you sent the letter out without having all the facts, and without asking us first, we may have a lot of explaining to do around here. That's all."

"Looks like we have a big mess to clean up," Marley said.

"Yup," I said. What else was there to say?

Jake and Marley still wanted their ice cream. While we waited, we could hear people gossiping about the story. Every table had a paper on it. People were pointing and ooh-ing and ahh-ing. It was nuts.

Dad grabbed two copies of the paper and sat at a table near the front door. We huddled close together to read the paper over Dad and Mr. Melton's shoulders.

"Do you see that?" Jake poked the paper with his index finger. "They're talking about us in here. And out there." He pointed at all the people in Myron's. "The article says that three local kids spotted what seems to be a creature in the lake. Check this out." Jake showed us the small print under the picture. It read: *Lake Bomoseen's very own "Bo" will be creating the Bomoseen Buzz this season.*

Dad raised his eyebrows. "Humph. Interesting. Listen to this," he said. "It says that they receive several sea monster claims with pictures each year, but they can usually be explained away." He cleared his throat loudly. "Look here. It also says a local diver has often been mistaken for a sea creature when he's in his scuba gear collecting golf balls from the bottom of the lake. See, I told you kids." He was about to close the paper when Mr. Melton put his hand between the pages.

"Wait, there's more." Mr. Melton continued reading. "What separated this sighting from others we've had in the past was the cover photo, which was examined by experts and could not be attributed to this diver. This may be a genuine sea creature. The photograph generated so much interest that we held up printing of the paper so we could get this story in our July issue."

Jake nearly spit his ice cream all over the paper.

"What?!" I shouted. "They think Sammy's picture is a genuine sea creature!"

Marley slapped the table, shaking all the water glasses. "This is so exciting! Maybe our plan can work after all."

Of course, my dad had to be the downer. "You know, in all likelihood, it still was Soggy Joe. Reporters always work the drama angle to get people to buy newspapers. So don't get your hopes up."

CHAPTER TWENTY-TWO
Bitter Sweet

When we got back to the cabin, I marched right over to Sammy and gave her a big hug. At first she was ready to karate chop me because a hug isn't usually the first thing on my agenda.

"Guess what?" I showed her the paper and poked my finger at the cover page, emphasizing each word. "Your picture made the papers!"

She squealed in excitement at first, but then cringed when she saw the sea monster picture on the front cover. "I thought it was my minnows."

Jake gave her a high-five. "It's even better than that."

Marley scooped Sammy up in her arms and gave her a giant kiss on the cheek.

Sammy flapped her hands and hopped like she had to go to the bathroom. "But I'm afraid of the monster."

"Wait, Sammy, listen," I said, grabbing her hand. "First of all, sea monsters aren't really monsters. They're just cool-looking sea animals that live under the water. They don't hurt anyone. They're just really rare. And your picture just might be what we needed to save the golf course for Mr. Melton."

Her face lit up. "Really? I helped? Can I run next door and tell Tyler?" Sammy didn't even wait for an answer before running out the door.

And that was the day it all started.

First people were buying papers, and the gossip hummed around the lake. Then more and more people showed up. Within a couple of weeks, the bait and tackle shop had lines out the door. The boat rental place ran out of boats by ten o'clock every morning, and people began renting houses that had been empty. Lake Bomoseen was getting more packed by the minute.

It was time to act. Jake and Marley agreed we should call a meeting with our dads and put Part II of our plan into action. We waited until morning when they would be getting ready for work and ambushed them at the kitchen table.

"Dad. Mr. Melton. Can we talk?" I asked, pulling out a chair. Jake and Marley pulled out chairs on either side of me. We had our serious faces on.

"What's on your mind?"

"Well," I started. "Since this whole sea monster thing has Lake Bomoseen lighting up like the Fourth of July, maybe you should think about our souvenir idea."

"You remember?" Jake added. "The hats. The T-shirts."

"Funny you should bring that up," Mr. Melton said, rubbing his bald spot. He reached down to his brief case and pulled out a sample cap, then a shirt, and then a cup.

Marley grabbed the cup. "Oh. My. Gosh. You did it!" she blurted. "You used our idea? This is awesome!" The cup had a cartoon picture of a sea monster. The cap had a picture, too.

Jake pulled the shirt over his head. "This is sick."

"But wait," Mr. Melton said. "We'd like you kids to come up with some sayings that we can print on the items."

Mom and Mrs. Weber came into the kitchen. Tommy pointed at Jake's shirt. "Monsa. Monsa."

"This is wonderful!" Mrs. Weber shouted, examining the shirt on Jake.

Mom clapped Tommy's hands together. "This is so exciting."

Mr. Melton started, "If you kids can come up with the slogans, we can get the items into the pro shop within a week."

"Okay," I said. "How about, *Bo Rocks Lake Bomoseen?* Or, *Lake Bo-moseen.*"

"Monsa, monsa!" Tommy shouted. We cracked up.

"That's a great one, Tommy! You kids keep working on those," Dad said.

"In the meantime," he continued, "the biggest news is that Bill and I decided to buy the golf course from Paramount Point. I've been looking for something to invest in, and we decided to become partners. I'll be a silent partner since we don't live here all year round, and Bill will stay and run it like he does now."

"GET OUT!" I blurted. I was so happy I thought I would explode from the inside out. "Dad, this is awesome."

"And," he continued, "We're going to upgrade the café in the pro shop as well."

"Really?" Marley said.

I could tell Mr. Melton was eager to talk. He rubbed his hands on his pants. "Yes. Since this deal includes the pro shop, I'll be running that with Peg." He motioned over to Mrs. Weber.

Jake looked up in shock. "Huh?" At first he looked a little wary.

Mrs. Weber cleared her throat. "Well, honey. During the summer months when you normally stay with your father, I can be in Vermont and run the café, or we can work it out so you can come up for the summers with me." She waved her hand in the air. "We can work out the details later. I spoke to your father, and he's very excited about it, too."

Mr. Melton continued, "The café will specialize in breakfast and lunch, and it will feature Peg's famous treats like the blueberry muffins. Of course we'll hire and train people to make all the recipes when she's not here." Then he took her hand. "Peg and I will make a good team."

Jake sat for a minute without saying a word. Then a big smile crept up on his cheeks. "Our very own café?" he said. "That's pretty cool!"

At first I was a little jealous that Jake was gonna get to hang out with Marley way more than me since his mom and her dad were a couple now. But then, duh! It hit me. My father was part owner of the golf course with Mr. Melton now, too. How cool was that? And Jake might get to be here with me during the summers. That was the best news of all. At least until Dad told us the next part.

"Kids, are you ready for this?" Dad paused and everyone was silent waiting for what he was about to say. Even Mrs. Melton and Mom didn't seem to know what he was about to tell us. "Bill and I loved the mini golf course idea, and we've looked into the permits we need. We were approved to start excavating the back half of the main golf course as soon as possible."

"Oh my gosh!" Mom shrieked. She ran over and hugged Dad. "That will definitely generate a lot of business."

"Exactly," Dad agreed.

"Yes!" I shouted. Jake and I high-fived. Then I high-fived Marley. I think I saw a spark when Marley's hand touched mine.

"There's more," Mr. Melton continued.

"Still more?" Marley asked.

"What else?" I could barely contain my excitement.

"Since you kids came up with the idea," Mr. Melton went on, "how would you like to help us brainstorm design sketches for the holes?"

The kitchen filled with screams and howls. "This is so awesome, Elliot!" Jake said. "You're... you're the best!"

Mom poured glasses of orange juice, and Mrs. Weber handed them out. "This calls for a celebration. And a toast!"

Sammy burst through the door with Tyler. Everyone took a glass and we all cheered.

"Here's to Sammy," I shouted, "for taking the best picture of Bo."

"Here's to Marley for an awesome letter to the paper," I said.

"And, here's to that girl Cassie," Marley added, "who came up with the original idea that got us going in the first place. She's okay, that Cassie."

"And," Dad added, "to my son, who's really grown up quite a bit lately, and for his efforts with his friends in coming up with some excellent business ideas. Thanks to you, my manager thinks I'm some kind of miracle worker."

The kitchen swelled with cheers and the sounds of glasses clinking. I felt myself blushing. I knew my face was as red as a fire engine. It was so awesome to think my dad thought of me as more mature now.

But then the orange juice churned a little bit in my stomach. I couldn't help thinking about all the stuff that Dad had said about the pictures. I thought about when he was examining them so closely on the laptop that his nose was on the screen. Most of the pictures we had did look like that guy Soggy Joe. I drifted off with my worries.

What did we do? What if it really was Soggy Joe? And then what if people found out that there really wasn't a sea monster? Then what? Would I be responsible if the whole thing fell apart? What if people thought we were lying?

I guess I shouldn't have worried because the golf course business continued to grow. When Jake, Marley and I weren't designing holes for the new mini golf course, we were helping Mr. Melton in the pro shop. We had come up with the best slogans for the souvenirs, too. The most popular ones were: *It's Bo, Not Joe* and *Monsa! Monsa!* Bo hats and Bo shirts, Bo candy bars, Bo postcards, and even Bo golf bags were flying off the shelves faster than we could replace them.

We helped Mrs. Weber in the new café. And guess what Marley did? At noon she would set up a little chair by the window and play her guitar. I couldn't believe how many people came to hear her at lunchtime. Me and Jake sat down to listen to her too. People even gave her tips. Her tip jar filled up faster than Sammy's Save the Minnows jar. She was *that* good. Cute AND talented. Nice! That summer, the three of us had become inseparable.

The bad part was, it was already the end of August, because we stayed longer than we were supposed to so Dad and Mr. Melton could get the golf course and pro shop going. Well, staying longer wasn't the bad part. The bad part was that now it was time to leave. And I didn't really want to go.

CHAPTER TWENTY-THREE
Sea Monster Cove

I decided I wouldn't worry about the sea monster thing too much, even though I still felt a little guilty knowing that it could very well be Soggy Joe sightings and not a real monster. But I figured people liked the idea or they wouldn't be in a frenzy buying up all this stuff. It worked just like in Scotland with the Loch Ness Monster.

Jake and I had instant messaged Cassie a bunch of times since all this started. She was totally psyched that her idea had helped us out so much. I even told her that Marley loved it.

I think the four of us could really be a great team. If Jake, Cassie, and I were the peanut butter, jelly and bread, then I wondered what Marley could be. The milk? *Hmmm. I'll have to think about that.*

We would be leaving in a little while, so Jake and I logged on one last time to talk to Cassie.

She popped on right away.

ClassyCassie5: HEY GUYS whats up?

Elliot1020: Just packing to go.

ClassyCassie5: I got my classroom number today in the mail. I got Mr. Bellray!!!

"Oh man, she's so lucky," I blurted.

Mr. Bellray is the coolest teacher in fifth grade. You should hear the stories. He's always playing pranks on Ms. Matson across the hall. I heard that one time he unscrewed her phone, so when she picked it up to answer it, all the pieces fell apart. And another time, he put a fake bug on her desk, and she screamed so loud you could hear her across the hall. He's so funny. And he's the chess team coach too. I love chess.

"Hey, Elliot." Jake had his I-have-an-idea face on. "Who's been picking up your mail while you guys are away?"

"My grandmother. Why?" I asked.

"My dad is picking up ours. Tell Cassie to call my dad and your grandmother and see if we got the same teacher."

"You are stuperpendous!" I said. I knew Jake would appreciate that word. He smiled.

After about twenty minutes, Cassie finally came back on.

ClassyCassie5:   YAY!!! You guys both got Mr. Bellray too!!!!

Jake and I jumped up and high-fived. This was gonna be a great year for sure! A great summer and a great school year. You can't ask for more than that. *Unless we could get Marley to move to New York and get in our class, too.*

We logged off and helped Mom pack the car. We waited for her outside while she took care of the last minute things. Jake was coming home with us because Mrs. Weber was staying back with Dad for a while longer to work on the business with Mr. Melton.

Sammy ran out of the house, and Mom and Tommy were right behind her. Roxy barked and bounded up the hill, right on schedule. She nudged me, wagging her stump of a tail. I patted her head, careful not to get drooled on. "Thanks for barking that day, Roxy. You're the reason Sammy got that awesome picture in the first place," I said. "Good dog."

Marley came out of her cabin and ran over to us to say goodbye. I felt a little weird because I wanted to hug her or something, but I didn't want to seem like a doofus.

She reached her hand out to me. It looked like she was holding something. "I meant to give you back the bracelet," she said. "Sorry. I forgot I had it on."

"Oh, uh. No, you can keep it," I said. "It matches all your orange stuff."

Sammy looked at it. "THAT's why you gave me that dollar," she smiled. "You bought a bracelet for Marleyyyyy."

I looked at the dirt, and I nearly burned a hole into the ground. Then I glanced up to signal Sammy to be quiet, but I saw Marley smiling, so I just let it go. It is fair to say I think I was melting.

"Thanks, Elliot," Marley said. "For everything."

I stared at my feet. "Aw, it was nothing."

Mom told Sammy to get in the car while she buckled Tommy in. Then Marley reached out and gave me a really big hug. I think I heard fireworks and explosions going off in my head. Kind of like the ones you see in cartoons. She hugged Jake, too (not as good as my hug, of course), and then she gave me a piece of paper with her e-mail address on it. *Jackpot!* When I took it from her, I could swear she squeezed my hand. I nearly keeled over.

Jake and I climbed into the third row in the back of the car, buckled up, and Mom drove away.

Marley waved as we bumped down the gravel driveway. I was so happy that I had her e-mail address. I definitely was not going to lose touch with her.

As we traveled down Fish Hook Lane and then onto Lake Willow Road, I stared out my window and thought about our vacation.

Mom cleared her throat. "Dad asked us to drive past the golf course on the way out. He has a surprise for you two."

We pulled into the parking lot and saw them instantly. Toward the back end of the golf course, big yellow bulldozers were tearing up the ground. Dad and Mr. Melton met us by the car.

"Surprise, boys! We broke ground today. The mini-golf course is on its way. We figured we'd show you now on your way out, and we'll bring Marley down later."

Jake and I cheered, "Alright!"

"By the time you get back here next summer," Dad said, "we'll have a fully running Sea Monster Cove."

"Wooohoo!" Jake howled. Even Sam and Tommy squealed at the good news. We all laughed.

Dad leaned in the window and kissed Mom. "Be careful driving. Call me when you get home."

We pulled out of the lot and continued around the lake. I checked out the boat rental place and the bait and tackle shop. They were both really busy, too. It looked like all the businesses were back to life.

As Mom stopped for a red light near Myron's, Tommy pointed out his window. "Monsa! Monsa!" he babbled.

I rammed into Jake so I could look over the seat and see what Tommy was pointing at. The familiar black neck emerged from the water. Jake's mouth was frozen open. I was afraid to blink and miss anything. People on the edge of the lake started pointing at it too, so I knew I wasn't crazy.

I spun around the other way and looked out my window to see if Soggy Joe's was open. And sure enough, there was Joe behind his table setting up more golf balls. It definitely wasn't Soggy Joe. It had to be a real sea monster. I shushed Jake, in case he was about to say something because I didn't want to scare Sammy. She'd been through enough. Then I watched the three humps ripple over the water. The sea monster seemed to be looking right at us. I held my breath until the traffic light turned green. And as we drove away, Bo sank beneath the surface.

 **LP Chase** is a children's author and freelance writer. Initially known for her middle grade mystery series, beginning with *Elliot Stone and the Mystery of the Alien Mom*, LP Chase has gone on to publish several other works of fiction, including *Elliot Stone and the Mystery of the Backyard Treasure*, *Today is Tuesday*, and most recently, *Silly Spoon*. In her spare time, she enjoys spending time with her husband and three children, exercising, reading, and baking. Chase resides with her family in Smithtown, New York.

 Carl DiRocco has illustrated several books, including *Our Principal Promised to Kiss a Pig* (a Children's Choice Selection) and *Dear Big, Mean, Ugly Monster* (a Minnesota Humanities Book Award finalist). Carl lives in Reading, MA with his wife and three sons. They love to vacation in Vermont.

Other Books by LP Chase

- *Silly Spoon*
- *Elliot Stone and the Mystery of the Alien Mom*
- *Elliot Stone and the Mystery of the Backyard Treasure*
- *Today is Tuesday*
- *The Ultimate Purple Notebook, Educator's Resource Guide,* By LP Chase and Joyce Gilmour

Children's Books Illustrated by Carl DiRocco

- *Madison's Patriotic Project*
- *Madison and the Two Wheeler*
- *Our Principal Promised to Kiss a Pig*
- *Make Sense! (Silly Millies)*
- *Dear Big, Mean, Ugly Monster*